These are the Rules

PAUL MANY

These are the Rules

Walker and Company
New York

All the characters and events portrayed in this work are fictitious.

First published in the United States of America in 1997 by Walker Publishing Company, Inc.

Published simultaneously in Canada by Thomas Allen & Son Canada, Limited, Markham, Ontario

Library of Congress Cataloging-in-Publication Data
Many, Paul
These are the rules/Paul Many.
p. cm.
Summary: Having quit his school's swim team, Colm tries to swim the lake at his family's summer home, at the same time working on his difficult relationship with his father and pondering the mystery of girls.
ISBN 0-8027-8619-7 (hardcover).
[1. Fathers and sons—Fiction. 2. Swimming—Fiction. 3. Self-confidence—Fiction.] I. Title.
PZ7.M31954Th 1997
[Fic]—dc21 96-46324
CIP
AC

Book design by Jennifer Ann Daddio

Printed in the United States of America

2 4 6 8 10 9 7 5 3 1

Once again
to
Zoe

Practically, the old have no very
important advice to give the young.

—Henry David Thoreau

As of Right Now

The windshield wipers are flapping, slap, slap, slapping: "You/screwed/up/good./You/screwed/up/good./You/screwed/up/good. . . ."

They're only saying it because it's true. Search your computer under "screwup" and you'll see my picture pop up on the screen.

Consider: I just get my driver's license and put my future ex-dad's car in a ditch. Another guy drives off with my future ex-girlfriend. I find myself hitching in the rain, then mashed in the jump seat of this station wagon with a bunch of kids and a big wet dog who's been rolling in . . . what? Smells like maybe putrefied whale droppings? I know it's raining, but crack a window, willya?

"Here OK?" The dad who picked me up reminds me of my own father, the way he Keeps His Eyes on the Road at All Costs. It's another half-mile walk, but it will put off the confrontation that much longer. "Yeah, thanks," I say. And all too soon, I'm at the house. Lights off; nobody home. Momentary stay of execution. After a while of waiting, I suit up and sit out lakeside.

Trust me on this. . . . Like you, I'm mostly interested in doing things right—the first time if possible. Call me lazy, but I've found it's really easier in the long run. But who can tell you anything about it? I only wish that life came with the rules printed inside the box. Then, if I ignored them, at least I'd know who to blame for getting into this mess.

The humid dark settles down around me and melts into the water. I think how good it would feel to be swallowed up in it all. I take off my shirt and wade in.

One

Did I ever tell you that last summer was *the* last summer I would spend at White Sand Lake?

Well, I was lying.

You would think that someone who was a junior in high school would be able to find a job. Then he wouldn't have to hang all summer with his mother and twin kidlings in some dumpy cottage with a toilet you could flush only once a day. And no driver's license.

But if you thought that, you wouldn't be thinking about me.

And I did have one all lined up—a job, that is—before my parents' separation. Don't get me wrong. I'm not blaming them. They were only doing what they had to do, as my mom says. My dad arranged it for me, but when I didn't see him for a month back there, and with all they were going through, I guess he forgot to call back his contact. By the time he remembered, somebody else was already drawing the paycheck.

He never forgot anything important, and it was exactly then I realized that since quitting the swim team, I was getting smaller and smaller in his rearview mirror. I couldn't have even *thought* about staying with him in his apartment in the city that summer.

Then, the first week out at the lake, Uncle Junior sees me shooting baskets at the hoop I nailed to the tree across the road from the cottage.

"Hey, Colm!" he shouts from his car. "You want to make a few bucks?" And next thing I know I've got a job after all, working for him, drilling wells.

He had a drilling rig he called the Hog that he'd welded up himself. It was like a tow truck, except with a higher boom, and he hauled the thing from job to job, since it wasn't street legal. When we got wherever we were going, he'd jack up the rear wheels, one of which had a two-foot cylinder sticking out from its hub.

Follow me closely now.

Around this cylinder he'd wrap a rope that went up over the top of the boom and was attached to a big weight. He'd let me start the truck, which always kicked in like a bomb, blasting flames out its tailpipe. Every time he'd jerk on the rope, it would tighten on the spinning hub, and pull up the weight. When he'd let go, the weight would fall back down.

Simple enough.

My job was to prop up a piece of casing pipe in a special frame, so it stood dead-level upright, then stand back as he let the weight drop, pounding the casing a foot or two into the ground. Pound it all the way down, couple on another, pound *it* down, and eventually you hit water.

Sometimes with all that was going on at home, I felt like that big ugly weight was falling right on top of my head.

Uncle Junior, I should explain, wasn't really my uncle. It's just what everybody called him. "Everybody" being the big Pacetti family who owned three houses all next to each other all around the little cove our cottage was on. Uncle Junior—who was a brother of a couple of the women there—lived in one of the houses and kept the properties up during the winters.

He'd been hurt when he was younger—no one ever did say how—but his leg was all messed up, and he got around with one of those short, stainless-steel crutches with a forearm cuff on it? And he had a big Frankenstein boot on the bum foot. This didn't slow him down much. In fact, his big chest and arms made up for the leg. And in all the time I worked with him, I never saw anything he didn't simply *do*, so maybe that's why nobody ever said anything. After a while, I even forgot about it myself. Besides taking care of the houses, he always had a little something going on the side, like this well-drilling business.

I'd been helping him only a week when the Pacettis came out for the summer one Saturday, bringing all their kids and dogs and cats and big boxes piled on their car roofs like a traveling circus. There was a glow in the sky over our cove that night like the houses were on fire. I always thought of this as the real beginning of summer.

"Come on over for dinner tonight, why don't you?" said Uncle Junior the next day, and so I did.

It was already getting dark as I walked down the driveway past Uncle Junior's restored chromed Buick—one of the old ones that looks like it's frowning in front?—to the Big House, where the grandparents lived. I could see the backyard was all strung with lightbulbs and lit up like a used car lot, and they had a boom box outside on a table playing some kind of classical music.

"Hey, Colm, come on in, we just sat down." Uncle Junior let me in through a screen door that was cut into a big screened frame that took the place of the garage door. Uncle Junior built this himself so they could all eat in the garage that was around back and underneath the house, open to the lake breezes. And here was everybody already sitting down at a couple of picnic tables pushed end to end.

"Colm! Good to see you! Come on, boy. [*Loved* it when they called me that.] How ya been?" One of Uncle Junior's sisters, Tessie, who was about as old as my mom, pointed to a place on the bench opposite the table from her and I stepped in between a couple of cousins and sat down. One of the younger kids—there must have been six or eight of them—went for a piece of bread and Tessie swatted him with a loose hand.

"Hey! You wait for Grandma," she said.

Then everyone got quiet and the grandmother got going in Italian and they all of a sudden shut up and bowed their heads. The second she was done, the boy reached again, and got swatted away again. "Guests first," said his mother, passing me the bread. I pulled out a chunk and it was warm and crusty, not like that spongy white stuff we had at home, which I could take a whole loaf of and squash down until it was thin as a book between my hands.

Before I could say anything, Tessie had loaded a big double handful of spaghetti on my plate along with a brimming ladle of sauce and a half dozen meatballs. I'd never seen such a pile of food. Then she splashed some wine in the drinking glass in front of me, and filled the little kids' glasses with water from the dark green metal pitcher on the table.

"Eat," she said.

I started fighting to get some spaghetti on my fork, while Uncle Junior began telling what a good worker I was, and just as I rolled up a blob of spaghetti the size of a baseball, I realized everybody was looking at me. They all laughed and the little kid next to me showed me how to get a few strands at a time, using a spoon. I sipped some of the wine, glancing around as I drank from the glass, thinking maybe they gave it to me by mistake, but nobody seemed to mind.

They were all into their own conversations, some in Italian, and as I took sidelong glances up the table, I suddenly noticed one of Uncle Junior's nieces, Carmella, who was about my age. I nearly didn't recognize her. Last summer she had been only a little kid in overalls. Now, somehow, she got five years older. Voices stormed around her, but she sat quietly eating. She had dark eyebrows and eyes like big, black olives, sparkly in the lantern light, and when she caught me staring at her, a little smile curled up the corners of her lips before she looked away. I paid closer attention to my plate.

After dinner, the kids all raced out into the yard. They wanted me to play hide-and-seek, but I was too old for that. Carmella and the women started to clean up, and I started to help like at home, but they waved

me off. So I didn't know what to do, and I sat there for a while listening to the uncles. As Carmella was working around us clearing the table, she dropped a plate and it clattered to the tablecloth.

"Hey, be careful." One of the aunts appeared from the kitchen to take a look.

"It's OK, it didn't break," Carmella said.

"It was my fault," one of the uncles said. "I bumped her arm," and he winked at Carmella and she laughed.

"You finished?" she said to one of the men, Uncle Attilio—"Tilly" they called him—who still had a little food on his plate.

"Why, you hungry?" he said. "Hey, I hear you got a job now," he added.

"Yes," she said.

"Such a big shot, in the city," he said. "So how come you don't stay there on the weekends with your aunt Angela?"

"Mom wants me out here to help," she said.

"I think she wants you here so she can keep an eye on you."

The other men laughed.

"You're the one somebody should keep an eye on," said Carmella.

"Oooooooo," said the other men, laughing at Attilio now.

She looked at me, gave her shoulders a little shrug, and went out to the kitchen.

After a while, all the men, except for Uncle Junior

and the grandfather, went out to the back of the property where they began playing a game where you rolled a little wooden ball down a long, flat court they'd made in the dirt, then tried to get close to it with bigger wooden balls. It was called boccie, Uncle Junior told me later.

I watched them for a while, then walked around the yard looking at the beds for the vegetable gardens the old man had started. He must've worked at it all day, because there were already maybe fifty or more plants—tomatoes, peppers, eggplants, lettuce—all in neat, raised boxes with little handwritten signs, which is how I knew what they were, city boy and all.

When the tape on the boom box ran out, I suddenly noticed it got real quiet. I could hear Uncle Junior talking softly in the garage, and all the crickets going—so many that it was one continuous trill. Then I heard a clacking—plastic on plastic—and saw it was Carmella flipping though tapes before she popped one in the boom box, and some big, way-overproduced singer who was popular right then came on. You could hardly hear his voice with all the strings and everything. She had her back to me and one of her arms to her chest and the other held up and she moved as if she were dancing with someone. The way she had her head slightly tilted

back, lost in it all, I couldn't help watching.

Then, suddenly, she turned. I didn't glance away quickly enough, and she caught me.

"Colm," she said, slightly embarrassed. But she held my gaze.

"Hi," I said.

"You were looking at me at dinner, too," she said.

"I was trying to figure out who you *were* at first. You looked so different." She looked at me kind of funny. "Older, I mean," I added.

"Oh," she said.

The tape continued playing and she hummed along, lost in the music for a bar or two.

"So you're out here for the summer?" she asked.

"Yeah," I said.

"Well, you sound *real* happy about it," she said.

"Well, I was *supposed* to have a job in the city, but it fell through." I didn't want to get into the separation and my dad forgetting and all, so I left it at that. "I'm glad your uncle hired me, or I don't know what I'd do."

Right then, the first tune on the tape ended and another revved up, the strings bursting out like molasses from a dam, the singer guy floating down on a bargeload of echoing guitars.

"You like him?" she said, mentioning the singer's name.

"It's nice," I lied.

"He's so cool," she said. "I have all his stuff. You should see my room." She closed her eyes and moved her feet a little with the music like she did before. Then something seemed to occur to her.

"Hey, you know how to dance?"

"Not really," I said. I almost said I'd seen people dance on TV, but for once I had the sense to keep my mouth shut.

"I could show you." I would have tried to figure a way to say no, but the way she sounded, she'd be hurt, so I went along.

When I got close, she took my right arm and put it around her waist. "Put your hand like this." And she had me flatten out my hand on her back. Her blouse was thin and I could feel her warm skin underneath and the way her body moved in and out with her breathing. My pinkie rested against the top edge of her shorts.

"Now give me your other hand." She was a little taller than me, I suddenly realized, up this close.

"Wait a minute," she said, like she was reading my mind. She kicked off her shoes. Her feet were light brown, her toes pale.

"There, that's better."

We started to move slowly, just behind the music.

"Now, the big mistake guys make is that they think all you have to do is walk in a circle," she said, like this was all from some magazine article or something and she was remembering what you were supposed to say as you went along.

"First, you need to be a little closer," she said. "Here." And she reached around and pressed on the back of my hand that held her waist. Her breasts bumped into my chest. She didn't seem to notice.

"Now, follow me." And she took me through it, back and forth with the left foot, pivot on the right. It was a lot easier than basketball, but I couldn't concentrate on where my feet should be with her so near like that, and her head next to mine. I could feel her breath on my neck, and got a heady dose of her perfume—the same that was in one of those scratch-and-sniff ads in a fashion magazine my mom had. I thought of the picture in the ad: a couple sitting by a fire on a beach, looking tiny against the huge starry night sky. Once when I got a peek at Carmella I saw she had her eyes closed again.

We did the whole side of the tape like that, nobody bothering us, although I caught one of the aunts poking her head out of the back door from time to time, keeping an eye on things. When it was over, Tessie shouted out for Carmella to come in; she had some other work for her to do.

"You going to be out the *whole* summer?" said Carmella, ignoring her.

"I wasn't planning on it, but I guess I am now," I said. I only meant that since I didn't have a job in the city I had no other choice, but she smiled like I'd said something nice about her.

"I'm here every weekend," she said. "You heard
Uncle Tilly? I got a job during the week, but my mom

makes me come out. She says she doesn't want me alone in the city. I mean, if you have the time, why don't you come over and I could show you more. If you want, that is."

When I said I would, the ends of her mouth curled up in her tight, shy smile.

Later, as I stood in my own backyard, facing the lake, I could see the lights from her yard through the trees down the cove. Above the smooth waters were more stars than I ever remembered seeing. They looked like the little bubbles in a glass of soda.

Possibilities were opening I'd never dreamed of.

Rule 1: Be prepared for surprises.

Two

Next morning my throat was dry and I felt a little sick to my stomach. It took me a few minutes to remember the wine. I'd have to file that away for future reference, as my future ex-father would say.

And that strange feeling out under the stars last night?

I pulled on my swim trunks and a T-shirt and sandals—my usual summer wardrobe—and got the coffeemaker going. I still wasn't sure exactly how much coffee you put in the thing, but I was getting better at it, at least that's what Mom said before she dumped the last batch.

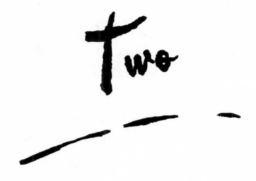

I ate a banana, then decided I couldn't wait for the whole pot, slipped my cup underneath the drip basket, held it there until it was half full, then switched back the pot. Didn't lose a drop. I threw in a couple of teaspoons of sugar and filled it with milk.

I sat out on the steps off the back porch, overlooking the lake, hoping the squawky screen door didn't wake up the twins, who would be all over me otherwise. I didn't get much sleep and still had a kind of glow from the night before and needed some quiet time to think. Sitting to one side were a basket of lawn tools and some packets of tomato seeds. Looked like my mom was going to get the plantings started a little earlier this year.

My dad usually did the garden. He always planted seeds at the beginning of July, which is why he only got a few tomatoes, maybe as big as marbles, before the first frost. This must've happened for the last five years in a row, but he always did it the same, anyway. He had ideas about the way things should be done, and never let reality get in the way.

I thought of Carmella's grandfather's garden and how his plants, surrounded by mounds of rich black dirt, were already as high as the width of my hand.

I saw Marlene next door, out on the back porch of her house "watching out" over the lake as usual. I told her once that she must have come from a family of lighthouse keepers. Hustling off to work like I was every day with Uncle Junior, I hadn't even talked to her yet this summer. She was someone else I'd lied to, I guess.

My mom had always winced at the first sight of

Marlene's house each spring. Everybody's from somewhere, and the Hackers happened to be from here. They had a washing machine out on the back porch, with a couple of car seats plopped down next to it, and a heap of rotten firewood. Marlene's mom worked nights as a nurse, and her dad worked days at a shingle factory, and Marlene and her brothers were free to whack baseballs up against the side of our house, or through our windows. Her older brother fooled with a four-wheel ATV, getting it going from time to time, and ripping around their yard getting their two rangy dogs all in an uproar, and kicking up clouds of dust that settled on the wash on our line or on our picnic table.

When my folks rebuilt the beat-up old fence between the two properties one year, they forgot to put the gate back in.

"Colm! You're back. I thought you said . . . ?" Marlene finally noticed me. Her voice sounded huskier than I remembered.

"It's a long story," I said.

Before I could say anything else she said, "You going to try the lake again?"

Last summer—way back when I was still on the swim team and thinking about a college scholarship—I got it into my head to try it. I'd been doing laps out to the raft and back, trying to keep in shape. Marlene came paddling by in her old canoe—some old green canvas fossil she'd found in an overgrown cove.

"What're you doing?" she said, as I held on to the raft, catching my breath.

"Practicing to swim the lake," I said, kind of pissed she was bothering me, and spitting out the first dumb thing that came out of my mouth.

Let me tell you a little about this lake: It was about two miles at its widest point and freezing until nearly September. People said it was bottomless, and that there was a big underwater cavern down there in the dark, where cold water pumped in from a huge underground river. There might have been something to this, since, although it had no outlet, the level of the lake rose and fell whether it rained or not like it had a mind of its own. There were always a couple of mysterious drownings each summer. Someone, almost always a guy, and usually in good shape, would dive off the side of a boat, and never come up. And nine times out of ten, people said, the body was never found, or came up somewhere in some lake in another state where by then it was a mushy blob, like white bread you threw in the sink. Maybe it was the streams of sudden freezing water you ran into every once in a while. I always imagined a guy cramped up like a rusted, knotty anchor chain, shooting straight to the bottom, where he got sucked into the backwash of that underground river. Even storms seemed to give the lake lots of room. You'd hear all sorts of booming and crashing and lightning special effects and then—nothing. It would all blow by. Sometimes it would even rain in town, but not out on the lake. Weird. And then there was my dad's phony story about some curse an Indian girl had put on the lake.

So let's just say that swimming that lake was the next thing I'd think of after windsurfing in the crater of an active volcano.

"Well, when you're ready, let me know, and I'll spot you," Marlene had said last summer.

"Yeah, thanks," I said, and kicked off of the raft.

But then every morning as I did my laps, she was out there in her canoe, reading her book, a drop line hanging off the side for perch. Finally one morning, I yelled out to her, "What the hell!"

I floated back to the shore, stood up in the shallows, and ran back in. "Here we go," I said. Same dumb thing everyone says before going on some killer roller coaster.

She paddled along ahead of me and to one side—far enough that she didn't get in my way, careful not to clunk the paddle. I could see her on my breath stroke, but after a while I even stopped looking and only listened to the whisper of her canoe as it cut the water.

I didn't get very far that first day, though, before I was beat, and she seemed to know exactly the right time to drop back to where I could get an arm over the gunwale and catch my breath. She said nothing, which was good, since I felt stupid already, and anything she said would have only made it worse. She paddled in, and I floated on my back, holding on, letting myself be pulled until we got close to the raft, where I said " 'Bye" and kicked off.

I stayed away from the lake a couple of days after that, but when I went back, there she was, waiting. After a few warm-up laps, I swam out, this time not even getting as far as I did the first time. Again, she said nothing, but the way she was there and helped out—it was the best kind of support you could get. By the end of last summer I had managed to swim more than half the lake.

But, like I said, that was way back last summer, a whole century ago. There was no way I would try it now.

"The lake?" I said. "I doubt it."

"Why not?"

"I'm not in any kind of shape, you know. I quit the team."

"You quit! Colm, what about college? Your scholarship?"

I thought it was strange she remembered all this about me. "Another long story," I said. "I don't feel like talking about it right now."

"OK," she said. You could see she was concerned, but she let it drop.

20 So we talked about school for a while instead. She was a year behind me, and I could tell her what to look

out for, but she was thinking about nursing school so there was only so far I could go. As she talked I noticed her face was—what can I say?—clearer. More distinct than I remembered it? She was somehow more *there*; not lost anymore in the doll dreaminess that still floated over the faces of younger kids like my little brother and sister.

Her mom yelled from inside the house for her to come put a diaper on her baby brother so he would quiet down and she could get some sleep.

"Some things never change," she said.

"Or always have to be," I said.

"I'm glad you came out," she said, looking me right in the eye.

I watched as she carefully picked her way back across the yard in her bare feet.

When the next weekend rolled around, I put on some long pants—which somehow made me feel older—and walked on down to see how Carmella was doing. As soon as I got there, though, I knew something was up.

Right in front of her house, at the end of a line of family-reeking cars—all outfitted with bicycle and luggage racks and plastered up with corny bumper stickers (WARNING: I BRAKE FOR NO REASON AT ALL)—was this candy-apple red, tricked-out ride with tinted windows, chromed wheels, oversize tires sticking out wide from the sides, the body chopped down low, and a set of subwoofers that took up the whole backseat.

I should have turned around right there, but instead, I went up the steps to the front door of the house and knocked. I waited awhile, but nobody came. The screen was open and I could see the rooms were empty, but I could hear people laughing around back, so I went down the driveway. As soon as I turned the corner of the house, I right away caught sight of this guy I hadn't seen before—not much older than me, but with his hair all chopped in some weird way and all dressed like on the music videos. You could tell he had some kind of ax to grind.

"Colm!" Carmella came up and took my hand and gave me a hug. "Good to see you," she said. "I was just telling Dean about the lake and all."

"Hiya," said Dean, extending his hand and giving me the Revolutionary Drug Brothers Grip—palms crossed and thumbs interlocked—like peace and love, man, you know?

"You from around here?"

"Only in the summers," I said.

"I told him how this place is dead," Carmella said.

"Yeah," I said. "Nothing much doing."

"You gotta get up to The Shores," he said. "That's not so far."

This was a place on Barstow Lake that had rides and a water park and a lot of burger chains and places to hang. It was forty-five minutes by car, but might as well have been on the coast of Portugal, with me not having my license yet, and, by the way, no car either.

I should say here that my mom is from a long line of people who lived in the city and had as one of the main teachings of their religion, "Thou shalt not drive." In the past she had counted on my dad coming out once a week at least to see us kids. Otherwise we walked or cycled to get stuff, or bummed a ride if we really needed one.

"Dean says he's going to take me up to The Shores later," said Carmella. She must have forgotten her invitation to me.

"Great," I said.

Then Dean showed us the car, which, from the way he talked about it, must've taken up every minute of his life with any time left over devoted to working in a mailroom so he could pay for it. The base from the subs rattled my molars.

"Great sounds," I said.

"Colm, you'll come in for something?" Carmella said, as we stood in the street looking at the car.

But I said, no, that I had to go, that my dad was coming soon. Which he was. I really didn't want to be back at the house when he *did* get there, but the way

Carmella and this Dean guy were looking at each other, I felt like they were going to give me a dollar and tell me to go buy some candy. So I had to get out of there.

And, sure enough, the minute I started walking home, whose car should I see coming down the road but my dad's. It was some old guy's idea of cool—some English convertible thing with the steering wheel on the wrong side—nothing like the brown, armor-plated box-cars he used to get. He went right out and bought it as soon as he and my mom got separated. I guess it was something he really wanted. I needed some more time to sort through all that was happening, and I hoped he hadn't seen me, but he must have, since he passed by our house and drove right up to where I was walking.

"Want a ride?" he said.

"OK," I said, and got in, hoping that Carmella and Dean weren't looking.

"How's things?" he asked, sticking out his hand to shake as he pulled into one of the Pacettis' driveways to turn around.

"Fine," I said, feeling strange shaking my own father's hand.

"I hear you lined up a job on your own," he said.

"Yeah," I said.

"How is it?"

"Good."

Then we rode in silence for the block or so to the

house. We didn't have that much to say before; why should we now?

"Here we are," he said when we got there. We went up the steps to the porch and my mom met us, not inviting him in any farther. She kept her arms folded, and he kept his hands in his pockets. It was funny to see them talk the way they did now. Not even like friends, but like somebody you meet in the supermarket and know from an old neighborhood where you used to live. The twins—I have a little brother and sister who are twins, if I didn't mention that—jumped up and hugged him, but I could see my mom was none too happy about that.

I guess when somebody's your father, you automatically make him look older, but now that I hadn't seen him in a couple of months, he looked a lot *younger* than I remembered, except around his eyes.

He said he was staying in a motel at the lake, and we could go swimming off the dock, and get pizza. I knew the place and believe me, there were so many condoms floating in the water there, it was like the Dead Sea—you hardly needed to move to stay up. Of course, he didn't mean to include my mom in this little trip, and just in case he had, she said, "I'm going to be outside, putting in the garden, so let the phone ring awhile if you call."

"I'm going to stay around here and help Mom," I heard myself saying.

He opened his mouth like he was going to say something to me, but didn't.

"Well, OK, then," he said to the kids. "You guys get suited up and I'll wait outside for you."

The twins roared off to their room to get their suits, and my mom and dad and I stood there.

"You're putting in the garden *already*," he said. "You know, you could still get a frost at night out here."

"I'll take my chances," said my mom.

"You're sure you don't want to come?" my dad said to me, more out of something to say since I think he was relieved at not having to take along his quitter son.

"No, that's OK," I said.

"I'll see what's keeping the twins," said my mom, going into the house and leaving us on the porch.

"Still sleeping out here, huh?" said my dad, looking through the screen at the fold-out bed that I hadn't gotten around to making yet.

"Yeah," I said. "The house gets too hot."

"I always told your mom we should get air conditioners."

"Yeah, but with the windows all closed up like that, you might as well be in the city," I said.

"That's what she always said, too," he said.

"I wasn't trying to take her side," I said.

"I know. I know," he said.

"Look, I wanted to tell you again that I'm sorry

about the job," he said. "I don't know where my head was."

I thought of a place but didn't say anything.

"Anyway," he went on, "I talked to the guy who I told you about and he said you could have it next summer if you wanted. But I'm glad you found something."

"Yeah, I am, too," I said. And we stood there inspecting the ants on the front steps until the twins came out.

After they left, my mom and I went around back to get the gardening stuff. I was surprised to see there were tears in her eyes.

Rule 2: Keep your eyes on the stars, but don't be surprised if you step on a banana peel.

Three

Some mornings as I sat out on the back porch I could see Marlene push off her canoe into the reeds at the edge of the lake. I guess this was her way of finding peace, drifting out there. I wish I could find something as simple that made me feel as peaceful, but it seemed the only way I could get to such a calm place was by wringing it out of me in sweat. Luckily, I had plenty of opportunity to take this option.

First of all, Marlene convinced me I should try again to swim the lake.

"But I've quit trying to impress people," I said.

"Who's talking about 'people,' " she said. "It's something *you* always wanted to do." It was hard to resist this logic, and with the clear early mornings on the lake, and pulling myself rhythmically through the clean water, and Marlene just being there . . . I've found you can get good habits as well as bad and I began to look forward to it. I mean, I really missed it on rainy days.

Now, between my long morning swims and long, hot afternoons lugging pipe for Uncle Junior, I should have cranked out enough energy to give me my daily "exorcism"—blow off all my worries, and beat me down into some calm, quiet pulp of physical exhaustion. I should have felt relaxed. But that summer I just couldn't get rid of it—that restless feeling, like when you put a bike in low gear too soon and you're pedaling and pedaling but not getting anywhere?

At least with my job I had the satisfaction of putting away a few dollars for school, but with swimming, like with most physical stuff, you couldn't plan on banking it. It was more up and down like the stock market (as my not-entirely-still-my-dad used to say). You shaved a second off your best time one day, but the next day it took you two *more*. Then, with the shark fin of shame slicing the water at your heels, you cut the two seconds again on the following day, so that in the end—you do the math—you finally netted out with that one second less you were looking for all along. Back when my dad was coaching me, if my time was off, or my form was no good on any one day, he would chew me out—call me lazy or accuse me of not caring. But I've learned at least one big lesson since I've quit (Yeah, there's that word again) and started working things out on my own: If you don't get all too excited or depressed about your particular performance on any particular day, but just concentrate on the goal, it all works out better in the long run.

One morning after my swim I was hanging on the side of the canoe. Marlene was reading and we were drifting wherever the currents took us. I was still wrestling in my mind with what I was going through with Carmella and needed someone to talk to, and Marlene *was* a girl, after all. I waited until I caught my breath, and was feeling revived enough to even kick a little and push the canoe. Marlene looked up.

"You know Carmella?" I asked.

"What about her?" she said.

"What do you think of her?"

"I don't know. We really never hung out together. With her it was always boys, boys, boys."

"And with you it wasn't?" I said.

"Not *that* much," she said. "Not then, anyway." She started to look at me but quickly looked away like she heard a fish jump clear of the water.

"What is she like?"

30 "I told you," said Marlene, who was still looking out at the water. "I was only with her a few times, like

we met in town or something. Why do you want to know so much?"

I was tempted to tell her, but for some reason instead I said: "I don't know. She just seems so different all of a sudden. Like she suddenly got *older.*"

"Well, all of us *did*, you know," said Marlene.

I didn't know whether she meant this as a joke or not.

"What would you be thinking of," I said, trying to come at it another way, "if you invited a guy down to see you and another guy was there?"

"Is this about Carmella still?"

"No, I mean, let's say, you."

"Me?" she said, thinking about it. She glanced at me. "How did this other guy get over there?"

"He drove."

"No, I mean, was he invited, too?"

"Maybe he just showed up."

"So I didn't invite him?"

"No."

"So why didn't I tell him to get lost, I was meeting someone else?" she said.

I thought about this for a few seconds. "I don't know. Maybe you liked this other guy, too," I said.

"More than *you*? . . . I mean the guy . . ." Here her tongue seemed to get all knotted like a snarled fishing line.

"I mean, I liked this *other* guy who just showed up more than the *first* guy I invited?" She finally reeled it out.

"Yeah, maybe," I said.

Now it was her turn to think. She kept her face turned from me. I noticed she had had her ears pierced since last year and wore earrings—small, gold sunlike disks—that caught little bursts of the real sun. "I guess I'd try to make the best of it," she said to the fish.

"You wouldn't feel like you owed the first guy something?"

"When you say 'invited,' let's go back to that. What do you mean? Did she ask this first guy for a date?" An earring flashed and now she was looking in my direction, although not at me.

"No. Just to talk; to come over, and see her," I said. For some reason, I didn't want to tell Marlene the whole thing—about the dancing and all.

"She said a time, and what you would do?"

"Would she have to?" I asked.

"If it was really something she meant, like something more *serious*"—she looked in my eyes—"like a date, and not just 'Why don't you come over,' she would."

"It *wasn't* a date, I told you."

"Well, then, I wouldn't feel like I owed him," she said. "It wouldn't be anything. I wouldn't be rude, but I wouldn't lead him on. I mean, I didn't promise him."

I thought what Carmella had said *was* a kind of

promise, though. But I couldn't figure out enough of the rules in this to even begin to ask any more questions.

"This is about Carmella and you, isn't it?" Marlene looked right at me as if my face were a page in her book.

"There's nothing *about* Carmella and me," I said. "Like you said: It wasn't anything. Right?"

"I guess," she said, turning away, grabbing her paddle, and with swift, sure strokes pointing the canoe back to shore.

I held on to the stern just behind her and she pulled me easily. There was a smell like baking bread or vanilla when you pour it out of the bottle that came off of her working like that, and—with the earrings and all—I realized it wasn't Marlene I was talking to at all.

It's like when I've come out here in the winter a few times, and was curious about what everything would look like, but it was so different, the snow on the ground and no leaves on the trees and all, that it just wasn't the same place. Well, suddenly it hit me it was like that with Marlene. She just wasn't the same tomboy with the scruffy pack of brothers from last summer.

Later that morning, I was out on the porch reading when my mom dropped a letter on top of the pages of my book. "For you," she said. The envelope was small and made of a crinkly, rose-colored paper. My name was in tiny, loopy handwriting, with the rest of the address
printed. It smelled of that perfume Carmella wore from the magazine. There was no return address, but it had a

city postmark. When I ran my finger under the flap to open it, I got a paper cut, but right away stuck the finger in my mouth so I wouldn't get blood on it.

"Dear Colm," the letter read. "Sorry we didn't have a chance to practice last weekend, but I'll be out again this week and you can have me all to yourself. Love, Carmella." First I got a feeling like the time when I was up in the loft of the old squatter's shack near here and my foot went through the floor. But then I cooled for a minute.

"Love." Maybe this was just what you wrote instead of "Yours, truly" when you got older? Or maybe she meant it. Maybe this Dean guy didn't mean anything to her after all, beyond a ride out to Barstow Lake. Maybe he was just somebody she knew from the city or a friend of one of the cousins.

Later on, over the roaring and lurching of the Hog, I asked Uncle Junior about what she was like.

"Carmella?" he said, flicking a glance away from the pounding weight for a second. "She was one of the first kids in the family," he said, shouting over the noise. "It's funny, you know how when other kids are born, the attention always switches to them—the littler ones? Well, not with Carmella. I guess it was self-defense. Get that cleanout hookup on, would you?"

I didn't realize the casing was already pounded all the way in and quickly set up the cleanout. This was a narrow pipe that fit inside the casing and had a sharp spade tip with two narrow slots just above for water to shoot out under pressure. When we finished pounding in a length of casing, we'd hook a hose to this cleanout pipe and use the rig to bang it up and down in the buried casing to flush all the dirt up and out.

"So what are you asking about Carmella for, anyway?" Uncle Junior said when we got another piece of casing going.

"I don't know," I said. "What do you mean by 'self-defense'?"

"Oh, just that. You see all the cousins around all the time? You have brothers and sisters, right?"

"Just the twins, and they're still kids."

"Well, Carmella has a little sister and a brother, too. But you saw at dinner the other night all the rest. We're just one big happy family. So there's lots of kids, and always were, and only so much attention to go around. But she was always the charmer. You saw her with her other uncles? Learned to do it right." He smiled and took a puff on his cigarette, leaving the rope slack for a few seconds, like he was thinking of something.

"Yeah," he said. "You look at the pictures of the holidays—you know, Easter and Christmas and everything?—and for every picture of the other kids there are three of her. She's got something. You should see all the boys at home."

"Boyfriends?"

He gave me a wary look. "I wouldn't call them that.

It's always just guys hanging around. She's too young to get serious. Louisa, her mother, wouldn't let her yet, anyway. Too young."

Well, this was positive news—kind of, anyway. Maybe this Dean wasn't a guy she was serious with. But I had a second thought—what do parents and uncles and relatives in general *really* know about what's going on?

The pounding of the weight and roaring of the engine from the Hog was pretty loud, and it was hard to talk so I let it drop.

On the weekend, I wore my jeans and an old shirt to go down to Carmella's. I wasn't going to set myself all up again just to get shot down. This time, only the usual cars were out front, though, and she met me at the door. She wore a big smile like this was all part of some conspiracy.

"Hi. You got my letter?"

"Yeah," I said. "Thanks." I tried to make it sound like it was just the letter I was thanking her for, and not that I thought it meant anything special.

"Come on in."

Off to one side of the entry hall was a living room that was closed off with sliding glass doors. I almost expected a fish to swim by, it reminded me so much of a giant aquarium. On the other side was a darkened dining room with a table spread with a cloth with tassels on the edge. Toward the rear of the house it was light, and we went back there into a big, bright kitchen.

"Ma," said Carmella. "It's Colm."

"Colm!" said Aunt Louisa. "Good to see you again. I'm glad to see you have such a nice young boy over," she said to Carmella. I could feel my face getting all hot.

"Ma, would you cut that out?" Carmella said. She rolled her eyes.

"Colm, you want some milk?" said Aunt Louisa. "Carmella, give him some milk and some of those cookies we brought from Scaturro's." And before I could say anything, Carmella sat me at the table and was putting a glass of milk in front of me and a pile of cookies on a plate. I wasn't used to being waited on, but she seemed to enjoy it. The ends of the cookies were dipped in chocolate and they were soft and melted in my mouth.

"Don't you get tired all week out here?" said Carmella, who sat down across from me. "What do you do when you're not working?"

"Oh," I said, "I go swimming—I'm . . . I mean, I've been swimming on the team at school, so I like to keep in shape, and I read and do other stuff." I thought I would leave it a little fuzzy and get around to telling her I quit some other time. It was all too complicated.

"Don't you guys have a car?" she said. "How do you get groceries?"

"No," I said. "My dad comes out on the weekends."

"I never see a car down there," she said.

I found it strange that she even looked for one.

"Well, he doesn't stay with us. You see, him and my mom are getting separated—they are already, I mean—and they don't stay together. He works in the city all week and stays down at the Lake Motel when he's here—he did the last time, anyway." I was finding it difficult to make sense. We both reached for a cookie, and her hand brushed mine.

"Sorry," said Carmella, looking right in my eyes.

"It's not so bad," I said. "I've gotten used to it. My mom has it worse off," I said.

"Ask him if he wants to go to the show with us," said her mother.

"Ma!" said Carmella.

"Well, why not? Colm, you come with us tonight. You can sit with Carmella."

"Ma!" she said, though she gave me her little smile. "You can, if you want to, you know," she said quietly.

"I guess," I said. "Sure, why not?" And I couldn't really focus on anything else she said that afternoon. All I could think of was sitting in the dark next to her.

Later, after supper at my house, I went down to Carmella's just in time to be herded into one of the big family buses one of the uncles drove (bumper sticker: MY OTHER CAR IS IN THE TRUNK)—one of the aunts riding shotgun. Uncle Junior was nowhere in sight. The car was packed with cousins, front and back. I sat next to the door, with Carmella squashed right up next to me. She slipped her arm through mine. "To save room," she said, smiling.

In the movie theater we took up pretty much of a row, with the aunt on one end and the uncle on the other. We were a couple of seats down from the aunt, who ignored us with all the commotion from the kids poking each other and spilling drinks, dumping popcorn and throwing stuff.

The movie was one of those big-screen action-romance things where a guy and some woman who hate each other have to find something with lots of jewels—some necklace—and everybody—good guys *and* bad guys—are chasing after them, and they have only twenty-four hours to find it, and you know the guy has got to fight every other guy in the picture while a whole dealership of cars gets blown up, and a few helicopters, and he finally wins the girl at the end. There may have been more to it, but I could hardly pay attention with Carmella so close.

As soon as the lights went out, she put her hand over mine on the arm of the seat between us. I turned mine over, so we were holding hands, and took a quick peek at her, but she kept her eyes on the screen like she was following every scene. After a while, my arm started going to sleep, so I let go and tried to put it around her, but she whispered "No!" and jerked her head toward her aunt. So I put my hand back on the seat arm, and Carmella squeezed it. She bumped my leg with hers, and I looked down to see her legs all pale in the light from the movie. Her shorts rode up an inch or two and I could see where her tan line ended. I tried to move our hands so they would rest on her leg, but when I budged them off the seat arm, she pushed them back.

Once she started shaking a little, laughing at all this, and her aunt bent forward to look at her, and Carmella immediately let go of my hand. But when the aunt sat up again, she held it as tightly as before. And once the aunt took a bunch of the kids to the bathroom and the old uncle was slumped down sideways in his seat, like maybe he got knocked cold from a jawbreaker—there were enough flying around. It looked like this would be a chance for something more, but when I tried to get Carmella's eye, she just kept looking at the picture, and it never went any further. The second the movie was over and the lights came up, she dropped my hand like it was a hot iron. She right away stood and began smoothing her clothes, tugging on the cuffs of her shorts to bring them back down. She talked excitedly about the picture the whole way home, like she hadn't missed much of it at all, and held her arm tight against her body, so I couldn't get my hand in. Her uncle, who had risen from the dead when the lights came up, stopped in front of my house first, so I had to get out, and she just said " 'Bye" along with all the others. The car slid off, silently, its red taillights shining more brightly as it reached her house. Then it disappeared around back.

Our house was all dark, except for a small light in my mom's room where she sat up—reading, probably. I was too confused and excited to go inside, however, and wanted to talk with someone for a while. I whistled, thinking maybe Marlene was at her usual post on her back porch, but got no answer. Maybe she'd gone in for the night, too, although she was usually up late. So I sat on our porch, swatting at mosquitoes that came in through the holes in the screen.

The lake was dark, with only a dock light or two shining dimly on the water. I thought I saw some movement off to one side, but couldn't be sure. Then I saw it—a canoe—a white canoe, flashing through a band of light, much closer to the shore than the motion I'd just seen. The hair on the back of my neck stood up.

Around many beach campfires for the many years we'd been coming out here, my father told a story of the native people—the Indians—who lived by this lake for thousands of years before the first white man ever laid eyes on it. Way back then, so my dad's story went, two tribes lived on opposite shores of the lake. One, whose name translated as the "Muckers," on the low side—our side—made pottery, and caught frogs and snakes to eat and dug up the cattails and other marshy plants. On the other side, where the lake fell off into deep water pretty quick, lived the "Fishers," who made their living catching fish and eels and collecting freshwater mussels.

The Muckers were traders—bartering the pots they made from the clay mud, baskets they wove from the tall reeds, and flour they made from the roots of the marshy plants. The Fishers, on the other hand, were hunters—so his story went—adding wild animals they caught to their fish diet, and making knives and fire starters from the flint on their more rocky shores. The two were such different kinds of people that for no other reason they became suspicious of each other, and eventually enemies.

One day a couple of Mucker sisters carrying baskets happened to run into a Fisher brave who had too many fish to carry. The plainer of the two sisters, who also happened to be the more generous, gave him one of her baskets and he gave her some fish, and a relationship was formed. Since the two clans didn't get along, the two lovers had to meet secretly. Finally, one day, they made a plan. On the next night there was no moon, he would swim out to the middle of the lake and she would meet him in her canoe and they would paddle off together.

42 Now, the Fisher Indian brave waited until the planned night, and, at first darkness, swam out to the

middle of the lake. But the more beautiful sister, who had overheard them and wanted the brave for herself, told her father about the planned meeting and he put the plain sister under guard.

The beautiful sister paddled to the middle as soon as she could slip away, but by then the brave had kinked up and drowned and she found only his feather floating on the water. She searched and searched the dark waters, but never found him. Now, this girl was very spoiled and used to taking nothing from no one, and when she couldn't have her man, she decided that no one else could have theirs. So she stood up in her canoe and raised her arms out and put a curse on the lake. Young men in the prime of their lives were to be the prime candidates for drowning. And now, on moonless nights, she still paddled those waters all in white buckskin in a white canoe, searching for signs of her drowned would-be lover, and drowning all the other young men she found. When I got older and read about the actual Native American people who lived here, I figured out that this was only some roundeye, gringo deal my dad cooked up to scare us from going too far out into the lake, or anywhere *near* the water in the dark, and was about as Indian as the Eiffel Tower.

I tried to see if I could catch another glimpse of whatever it was out there, but by now, judging by where it was headed, it would be in the darker shadows of the evergreens that lined that part of the lake. You could hide an aircraft carrier in that kind of dark, so I gave it up and let it go.

Rule 3: You can't always be sure the girl's going to be there when you swim out to the middle.

Four

I didn't get a letter or a phone call or anything from Carmella that week. I thought of sending *her* a letter—calling would just be too tricky—but I didn't know what to say. I mean, do you write "I love you" when you've just *started* to feel it? When you *think* you've just started to feel it? And was this the way love felt, anyway? I mean, it was really different, of course, than what I felt around my family.

Also, it was like I *first* needed to know that Carmella felt the same way for me. I mean, to know if I really did love her, I'd have to know that she loved me, too. But that was kind of weird. Did I love her or didn't I? Wasn't it *my* feelings we were talking about here? The more I thought about it, the more complicated it got.

Next Saturday, I went down to her house like nothing had happened at the movies and all, and it was the most natural thing in the world. Only the usual motorcade was out front, so that was a good start. Aunt Louisa—Carmella's mom—came to the screen door. She smiled but opened it only halfway. Something was up. "Colm, good of you to come. How are you?"

"Fine, Mrs. Pacetti," I said. "Is Carmella in?"

"Oh," she said, "but Carmella says to tell you she's not feeling so good today, and would you come back next week? I'm so sorry," she added. She looked like she wanted to tell me more, but didn't.

"Oh, OK," I said, as if it didn't bother me at all. But now I really *was* confused. Was she really sick, or did she just have her mom tell me to get lost? Maybe I should have waited longer to call on her? But it was a whole week. Maybe I didn't try hard enough at the movies. But she was the one who had pushed me away. Maybe I should have sent a damn letter. And why did Carmella already tell her mom to tell me she wasn't feeling good? She must have expected I would come down. I knew this was going to be worse than calculus.

At home, the twins were all excited about Dad coming out again for the weekend. He hadn't missed one yet.

"Colm! Dad's taking us to The Shores today," said Robbie, pulling on my arm.

"Yeah!" said Marie. "We're gonna go on all the big rides."

"We'll have to see about that," said my mom. "Colm," she said. "I thought you were going down to Uncle Junior's?" This was my cover story.

"It didn't work out," I said.

"Why don't you go with the twins, then," she said. "I'm sure your father would appreciate the help. And you know, just because your dad and I—"

"I know, Mom," I cut her off.

"Anyway, I'd like to see you two talk more, like you used to."

I was going to remind Mom that, since the swim team fiasco, we *hadn't* talked all that much, but then it hit me that maybe going with Dad might be some sort of way of getting *them* talking more again. You know, "How about that Colm? You know what happened today?" And like that. So I said I would go.

Just one of the kids again.

Dad showed, right on time, but Mom didn't even come to the door. She heard him pull up and honk the horn and she kissed the twins and gave me a hug and sent us all out.

"Well, *Colm*!" said my dad, as I got in the car. "What a surprise! I'm glad you graced us with your presence. What happened? Your mom let you have the day off?"

I knew what he was like when he got like this, so I just said, "Yeah," instead of getting into it with him. The twins started blabbing away, so I couldn't get a word in after that anyway and just sat there watching the road stands and farms and fences go by.

Barstow Lake must've been around for a hundred years. I mean, the lake itself was *thousands* of years old, of course, but The Shores, the amusement park and campgrounds that were set up around it, looked like they were coughed up like some giant hairball by the last glacier. The place was built back when cars first came in and, at the time, it was a good morning's drive by horse and carriage or Model T from the city instead of the hour or so it is now. Everything was old and rickety and built with a lot of wood and held together with what Uncle Junior calls "a half inch of putty and a quarter inch of paint." The roller coaster, for instance, was this big pile of beams and stuff, and looked like one of those old bridges across a canyon that gets blown up and the train goes flying off into the valley?

The merry-go-round was inside a round house that was painted blue and white and orange, and a lot of the other rides were in what looked like buildings. But once you got on them, you could see these were all just false fronts propped up with two-by-fours like stage scenery. Some of the rides were halfway taken apart and closed.

The twins ran all the way from the parking lot and Dad and me had to hustle to keep up with them. They

wanted to go on their favorites right away, but Dad insisted they do it "the way you're supposed to" and start just inside the gate and go around—the same way he always made us do it. "So that when you get tired later we'll already be back by the gate again, and I won't have to carry you."

The twins were fearless. A lot of the rides I wouldn't go near even now, never mind when I was a kid their age, they went on twice. One was this wheel that started out level, but turned up on its side so you were squashed against the edge and upside-down half the time. Dad liked the rides, too. Or at least he made out he did. He was walking kind of wobbly when he got off a few, but when they wanted to go on again, he said "No problem," and they all did it again.

Now, I can take going around and around forever, and even up and down, but put the two together and it makes my lunch get its own ideas about where it wants to be. It's not like I'm scared or anything, but performing the Big Spit for a crowd of admirers in a packed park is not my idea of a spectator sport. So I begged off on a few, although I knew this would become one more verse of "The Many Ways My Oldest Son Let His Daddy Down"—soon to be a country song at a record store near you. I was relieved, though, when we finally got to the bumper cars. Flat on the ground! Here was something even I could handle.

Like all the other rides in the place, this one was beat. It stank of grease and oil, and Marie somehow got some black stuff all over the leg of her pants just standing in line. A bunch of cars were pushed over to one side and covered with some old pieces of canvas, and the ones that were working were all scraped and scratched and dented up, except for one Robbie made a beeline for, which was first in the line of stopped cars and all shiny and new looking. As I got in it with Robbie, I realized it was only the paint that was new, and that whoever painted it got it on the seat and steering wheel, too. I couldn't get Robbie's seat belt to work, so I kind of stretched mine over both of us, but we were held up, anyway, while I was doing this, by a big bunch of people who came running in at just the last minute.

A buzzer buzzed and the guy running the ride threw the switch and all the cars jerked into action. Sparks rained from where the long poles from the cars scraped along the ceiling.

"Come on, Colm! Go! Go!" Robbie started yelling at me. We had no one ahead of us for halfway around the course. My dad and Marie were in a car right behind us and gaining on us, and everyone else was behind them. I had the accelerator pedal smashed to the floor and was turning the wheel one way and the other trying to get us going, but nothing was happening. Then my dad's car rammed into us, Marie squealing and laughing, and we went spinning.

The steering wheel had a mind of its own about

where the car was going, and the accelerator was either off, or on full, so we spun and lurched all around the floor, not going much of anywhere except when we got blasted by another car. I thought I heard a laugh I knew, and sure enough, coming right at us was a car driven by Dean with Carmella holding tightly to him.

"Watch out!" she was shouting in between laughing. "Get out of the way!"

She had to see it was me, but she acted like I was somebody she didn't know. The car hit us broadside and we got flung into a corner next to the busted cars and everybody zipped around behind us as I turned the wheel back and forth and mashed the pedal, trying to get the thing moving. Then the buzzer went again, and all the cars stopped.

"Colm! What were you doing there?" said my dad, looking almost mad as we walked over the steel floor to the exit. I tried to tell him it wasn't my fault, that the thing wasn't working right.

"Ours worked good!" said Marie. "We really knocked you guys silly," she said, bumping into Robbie, who was scowling.

"You can't turn the wheel so sharp," said my dad, "and you have to feed it the gas slowly at first."

"There *is* no gas," said Robbie. "It's electric. Next time *I* get to ride with Dad," he said. I knew it was useless to try to explain any more, so I didn't.

I saw Carmella, waiting on line to go in again, and I

dropped back to say something to her. Maybe she hadn't recognized me.

"Colm!" she said, though, right away when she saw me. "You remember Dean?"

"Yeah," I said. He gave a little wave.

"Sorry I was sick this morning," she said. "My mom didn't tell you I got better? Dean came out anyway. He was going to drive me over here."

"Yeah," said Dean. "Looks like you don't drive so good, yourself," he said, jerking his thumb over his shoulder to the ride we just got off.

"The thing wasn't working right," I said. "See? It was that blue one." I pointed out the brightly painted car. "Don't take it."

"Thanks for the tip," said Dean, but right then, the line started to move.

"Give me a call," said Carmella, as they got swallowed up into the ride.

Dad had nothing much to say to me the whole rest of the time. I could see he was mad. Yeah, it was only a ride, but try telling that to my dad, whose motto was "A game is *only* a game the way life is *only* life."

Besides, the twins took up all his attention, getting cotton candy on their clothes and stepping in ice cream, and finally getting tired and crabby when we weren't even halfway around, so he had to wind up carrying Marie back all the way anyway.

On the way home, the kids slept and I pretended to, so I wouldn't have to try to talk with him.

Rule 4: It's hard to steer when you don't know where you're going.

Five

"It's simple," Marlene said after I told her about the bloodbath at Barstow. "You have to learn to drive." Marlene had a way of taking a puzzle and right away picking out the frame pieces that made it all start to fit together.

"Then you could make your own decisions," she said. "You could call the shots. You wouldn't have to tag along with your dad or the kids. You could drive Carmella yourself, and forget about Dean."

We were out in the middle of the lake—about as far as I was able to swim so far—me floating around on my back, Marlene drifting in her canoe.

"That's probably what Carmella is trying to tell

you," she added, just as we drifted into one of the lake's famous cold eddies.

"*Trying* to tell me?" I said, with a shiver. "*Trying?* . . . Try to stand up."

"Me?" said Marlene.

"Yeah," I said. "Go ahead. Try. I'll hold the canoe."

"Right now? Well, I *could.* It would take a little balancing, but I could do it. What's your point?"

"That's my point," I said. "You do it or you don't. If Carmella wants something she should just tell me."

"Was it your dad or your coach who told you that one? Sounds like some kind of 'Can't means won't' crap to me," she said. Marlene never took a hit without coming back at you.

"But why *didn't* she just tell me?" I asked.

"It doesn't work like that," said Marlene. "You're supposed to figure it out." She said this so quietly I almost didn't hear her.

"Wait," I said, "I get it. I have to guess what she wants, but get punished if I guess the wrong thing. Right?"

"If she has to *tell* you," Marlene continued, "then you just aren't in tune with her."

"Now we're talking duets?"

"Yeah, why not?" said Marlene.

I gave up and tried something else. "Who's going to teach me, anyhow?" I said. "My mom doesn't know how and I don't have a car."

"Uncle Junior."

"He's got his car all rigged up with his homemade hand controls—only *he* can drive the thing, and anyway you know how old it is and everything? I don't think I'd want to, even if I could."

"So who does that leave?"

"Who? Nobody."

"Think about it," she said.

I thought for a few seconds. Suddenly it came at me the way you know a line drive is coming right at your head.

"No!" I said. "You've got to be kidding."

"It's your only way."

"My soon-to-be ex-dad?" I said. "The Taskmaster of the Universe?"

"Why do you call him names like that?" she asked, fixing me with a stare like I was one of the snakes that sometimes curled across the water. Her dad was different.

"Did I ever tell you about him and the swim team last year?"

"No," she said. "You said it was a long story. Go ahead. I've got time." She folded her arms and stared at me. So I swam over to the side of the canoe and held on and told her.

My dad had been a star swimmer in high school and college. There wasn't anything he wasn't good at: breaststroke, backstroke, freestyle—you name it. And half the damn trophies in the glass case outside his high school gym had his name on them.

Somehow I should've known better, I guess, but I was a little kid when he started teaching me. . . . It was out at the lake—this lake—where he first got me to swim out to the raft when I was really little. Mom was a wreck. And then, little by little, he showed me the "right way" to kick, move my arms, move my upper body and head—even to breathe. "No turtles!" —I still remember him shouting at me—"Get your head down in that water, mister!" Then he started timing me. It was like anything else: It happens a little at a time, and then all at once, and next I knew, it was halfway past high school, and I was beginning my junior year on the swim team, and not doing so bad, either.

But then I lost a couple of races and my dad wanted to have a meeting with my coach. He was a swimmer, too, back in college, but not as big time, and my dad was going to give *him* a few pointers.

Mr. Alfieri didn't take to it too well—my dad isn't exactly a diplomat at telling you when he thinks you don't know something. After a couple of times, Alfieri basically told my dad to get out of his face, and if he was so good at it, why wasn't he a coach, himself, instead of poking keys on a computer all day downtown? Well, that was all my dad needed, and he said that if the coach wasn't going to do it right, he would. Except he never told Alfieri that, but instead started coaching me himself.

So he took me three or four mornings a week—early, before school—downtown to his club, which had a big pool in the basement, and gave me tips and pointers. Except with him, you could never do it right. He never seemed to find anything good about what I did. It was always "You screwed up this and you screwed up that." If I beat my last best time, he would say, "You got lucky." If I was sore or stiff and it slowed me down, he said I was just lazy and didn't want to work. He'd set a workout for me and leave for a few minutes, then come back and yell at me for not having it done yet, or tell me two different things to do and yell at me for doing one and not the other. All this wore me out, so by the time I got to regular practice in the afternoons, I was exhausted.

Alfieri must have known something was up as soon as he saw me slogging across the pool halfway through practice, but he didn't say anything. Instead, *he* pushed me all the harder. So pretty soon it was like a tug-of-war between my dad and Alfieri, with me in the part of the rope. What used to be fun wasn't anymore. I told my dad I couldn't take it, but this got him all the madder and going on about not ever saying I couldn't; that there's no "I" in "team" and when the going gets tough . . .

("And 'Can't means won't,' " said Marlene with a smirk.)

Finally, one snowy Saturday morning in the middle of winter, I got to my dad's club and suited up and went out to the pool. My dad was back at the house after dropping me off, since he had to finish digging out the driveway and the walk. There was only one way to do this, of course—just when it fell; God help you if you waited until it got packed down. He was going to come and work with me when he was all done, and I was supposed to be warming up, which was just laps for a half hour or so, and he trusted I could do that right. The janitor had just turned up the heat in the pool for the day, and no one else was there when I walked out on the low dive and stood at the end looking down into the water.

I could see the shadows that the current of warmer water made as it billowed in like some invisible cloud, past the bright blue lane lines painted on the bottom. Standing at the lip of the board, I watched the swirls as they fanned out, trying to figure when most of the pool would be warm. The water seemed so peaceful, and I just stood there, looking, arms folded in front of me, swim goggles up on my forehead.

I stood like that for a long time.

And then, after a while, I just turned around and went back to my locker, got out my street clothes, and got dressed.

I walked through the snowdrifts to a diner down the street, and sat down and ate breakfast, and listened to people talking about the snow and what was in the paper and the counterman asking "The usual?" when someone new came in.

"So this is what normal people do," I thought as I watched the snowplows clear off the street. And I thought of all the opportunities I'd missed—going out with girls and on camping trips and just hanging out—and how emotionally challenged I was from focusing on this one thing almost all my life so far. After a while, a neighbor stopped in, and I got a ride home with him.

"Where did you go?" my father said when I walked in. "You were gone already when I got there."

"I'm through," I told him.

"What do you mean?" he said. "You couldn't have finished, it only took me a half hour at the most."

"No," I said. "I didn't practice at all. I'm not swimming anymore."

"Why not?" he said.

"You know that saying 'Get a life'?" I said.

"Yeah?" said my dad.

"Well, I'm going to," I said.

"You're going to throw all of this out? Ignore all the time and work I've put in to help you?"

60 "That's just it, Dad," I said. "It's all the work *you've* put in that you're worried about."

"That's easy," he said. "Make me the big, bad dad,

when *you* were the one all pumped up about being good enough for college and all."

"But I'm so exhausted I can barely study," I said. "I can barely do anything outside of swim. And let's face reality, Dad, I don't have a career ahead of me as a professional swimmer."

"Reality is what you make it," he said—another response from the Big Book of Coaching—as if none of what I said had any real meaning for him other than somebody trying to goof off.

We went back and forth like this, and finally he just shook his head and waved both hands in front of his face like he was chasing off a cloud of gnats, and walked.

He wouldn't talk to me for a couple of weeks after that. Some nights I could hear the mumbling behind the bedroom door as my mom argued with him after I went up to my room. I guess she was taking my side, which didn't help at all what was going on between them. And I can't help but think sometimes that fighting over me was the final straw in breaking them up.

"So what you're saying," said Marlene when I was through, "is that you think you've emotionally destroyed your mom by wrecking her marriage, and ruined your dad's plans for success in the world by wrecking his hopes in his first-born son."

"Real funny," I said.

"I'm just repeating what it sounds like," she said.

"You're trying to live your own life, in the way *you* think is best, and there's no crime in that. And if your dad can't take it, that's his problem. And your mom and dad, not getting along. Well, that's got to be another long story entirely."

She was quiet then for a while and we floated finally into warmer water. "But what does all this have to do with what we were talking about—getting you some driving lessons. Isn't the swimming thing history with your dad and you by now?"

"Are you kidding?" I said. "For my dad, it's history all right, just like this morning is history. It's just as fresh and new to him as the day it happened."

"You sure?"

"Well, I haven't asked him about it, if that's what you mean. And it's not just that, anyway," I said. "Even if he would agree to do it, I'm sure it would be the same old crap: 'Colm, you're not listening; don't stomp so hard on the brakes. Colm, I said *left, then* right. Colm, Colm, Colm . . .' If I wait until senior year, I could take driver's ed and . . ."

"And Carmella will be married to this Dean guy, and you can be the godfather of their first baby."

"Boy loses girl. End of story," I said.

"But not 'The End,' " she said softly.

 I looked up at her. She caught my glance, but quickly dropped it.

"Meaning?" I said.

"Meaning, never mind," she said.

"Well, forget it," I said. "There's just no way I want to have anything to do with learning anything from the guy," and I let go of the canoe, dropped underwater, and kicked out a couple of yards before starting to float back to the raft.

Later that afternoon, I put the situation to Uncle Junior, not telling him the Carmella part so much, but more about how since I didn't drive I felt like a kid and how in case of an emergency I should know, and all that.

"Well, you know I wish I could help you, but there's not much I can do," he said, rhythmically pulling on the rope and releasing it.

"So what would you do, if you were me?" I asked.

"Steal a car and practice on my own," he said.

"Come on," I said.

"What do you want from me?" he said. "Is it *that* bad with you and your father?"

"There's just no way," I said. "I don't know what yours was like . . ." I started to add, when, with a violent wrenching, twisting sound, the weight came loose from the casing pipe and landed on the ground, jerking the whole rig off its blocks, and pulling Uncle Junior off the upended drywall bucket he sat on. The truck stalled and was quiet.

I ran over to Uncle Junior, but he was already standing up and brushing himself off.

"Damn!" he said.

The piece of casing pipe was bent at an angle and the weight and yards of loose rope lay next to it.

"What happened?" I asked.

"She cut loose," said Uncle Junior. "The pipe must've been off."

The pounding weight had a narrow rod sticking out of it that slid into the wider casing pipe kind of like an arm in a sleeve. This kept the weight on course in its up-and-down motion as it pounded down the pipe. As Uncle Junior showed me, the casing pipe must've gotten bumped somehow and knocked off the ninety-degree perpendicular. The heavy weight falling on it bent it little by little until finally, with one of the blows, it doubled over, dumping the weight off on the ground.

We had a long level that I put next to the casing when we'd first set up the pipe, and now Uncle Junior pointed to it. "We'll have to slap the level up next to it every once in a while. We must've hit some rocks and that's knocking it off," he said.

We soon had the bent pipe dug out and uncoupled—fortunately it hadn't gone down very far—and a new piece coupled on and going.

After a half dozen or so slams with the weight, I tried the level on it.

"How's that?" I asked.

"Whack it a little to your right with that sledge," said Uncle Junior.

I gave it a couple of light taps.

"Keep going. More. More. OK. It's gotta be perfect," he added.

"You sound like my dad," I said.

"Sometimes you just gotta be," said Uncle Junior. "Maybe your dad is right."

"Are you kidding?" I said. "He's nuts. I remember decorating the tree at Christmas. We were never allowed to just throw tinsel on it. We had to put it on strand by strand."

"People pick one way and not another usually because they feel they *have* to," said Uncle Junior.

"But hey," I said, "people make their own choices; this is a free country."

"Not free up here," he said, tapping his head with a forefinger. "Where did your dad grow up?" he said.

"Some small coal town in Pennsylvania," I said, and told Uncle Junior some of the tales my dad had told me, which by now were like some old black-and-white movies I had seen so many times I could project them inside my head: The scene where he and his brothers slept four to a bed and "the first one up was the best dressed." All of them hunkering down around the coal stove, which kept the room warm about three inches away from its surface. He and his older brother scrounging in the woods for old soda bottles to buy potatoes so their mom could make potato soup. *His* father, the screwup, not a drunk anyway, but just not all there, coming home in the middle of the day after getting fired again. The curtains being ripped off the windows by the landlord when they got kicked out of yet another beat place where they lived, so they kept moving a couple of times a year. And all the rest of what I called his "covered wagon" days.

"And how did he get out of all of that?" asked Uncle Junior.

"He swam out," I said, explaining his swimming talent, and the long hours he put in, and how he got a college scholarship out of it.

"Don't you see," said Uncle Junior, "all of that wasn't 'Take it or leave it' to him. It was 'One way or die.' It was survival, man. He had to be perfect to get out; he had to be who he was. You can't fault a guy for that."

Maybe I couldn't fault him, but I wasn't going to deal with him.

And when I saw Uncle Junior was only going to take his side, I yessed him until he was satisfied and then let it drop. There was just no way I was going to let my father teach me to drive. Ever!

Rule 5: Everyone has his own life to swim.

Six

"*You rolled through that stop sign.* You're supposed to come to a *complete* stop!"

Dad wasn't shouting *yet*, but the top edges of his ears *were* getting red. I could tell this wasn't going to work.

On my own, I'd never be here, in his car—the swift and sexy soon-to-be-bachelor-mobile—learning to drive in it, no less. Learning *from my father*, no less. But last Sunday, after he left for the weekend and the twins were in bed, my mom busted out crying.

We were right in the middle of watching some Summer Olympics gymnastics thing where the little girl who was supposed to win—it was on the balance beam— some poor kid from one of those little countries in East

Europe where they have all the trouble all the time—just fell off.

First she was on it. Just taking a step on her way from one no-hands-impossible-double-twist-over to another. Just *walking* on the beam, which for her must've been like walking on the top of a dining room table. Then she was off it. Fell right off. Hard, too. She hit part of the equipment going down and her trainer had to rush out to see what was wrong. And they had to keep replaying it and replaying it, until they got her to her feet and she went on and finished out her routine. She was perfect, otherwise, but this blew the event for her.

And right then, when the low scores came up, with the camera stuck in the girl's being-brave face, my mom started bawling. Like I said, the twins were in bed already, all worn out from Dad running them around a miniature golf course and one of these indoor playground places in the mall.

I stayed home, hoping to catch up with Carmella, and I phoned this time, but she stayed in the city that weekend, so I wore off my extra energy just doing laps. Out to the raft and back to the shore, again and again. Marlene out in the canoe—a little dot out on the water.

I was tired after all this and kept nodding off at first, but then the Olympics caught my interest, and I thought I'd keep my mom company, anyway. You could see she was kind of lonely at times.

"What's the matter?" I said.

"Nothing. Nothing. It's OK," she said, blotting her mouth with a paper napkin. We were eating popcorn that she cooked on the stove, and the napkin was wet and blotched with butter. She finished chewing a couple of bites, the tears running down into her mouth. I sat on the arm of her chair.

"Mom," I said, "I know you're not losing it over this kid blowing her event. Tell me. What's wrong?" I could see she needed to talk.

"It's OK, Colm," she said. "I don't want to get you into this."

"But you're my mother," I said. "I *am* into it. It's about Dad, isn't it?"

She cried quietly for a while. "I guess I thought after I got over the shock of all this, things would be normal in a way. But it's all so hard," she said. I put my arm around her and hugged her next to me, awkward as it was sitting on the chair arm like that.

"Tell me, Mom," I said. "I'm old enough." I wasn't really sure if I wanted to hear.

"Well, your father, you know how he is," she said.

Only too well, I thought.

"He said that if he could only see you kids on weekends, he'd rather not see you at all."

"He doesn't want to see us anymore?" I hoped I didn't sound too happy about this.

"No. What he wants is to have them—you, too—

for *longer*—more than just the weekends. He seems to think that when you don't see him, you're starting to think bad things about him. Like he doesn't love you."

"Mom, I always had troubles with Dad," I said.

"But you always seemed to be able to patch things up and get along with him."

(The way Costello got along with Abbott, I thought. Whap!) But I said, "Dad has *always* been hard to get along with. I've *always* had troubles with him."

"But before this . . ." She started blubbering again, and I had to wait before she could say anything. "Before this, he said, you always made up."

"But this year, with the swimming and all, was different," I said. "This was more serious. *Way* more. And besides," I added, "there just wasn't that much time for it, so much was going on with you guys splitting and all."

"That's part of it, though," she said. "He says you just don't want to spend time with him."

"Mom!" I was getting exasperated. "It's not just *him*. . . . I'm getting older. I have my own life to lead. It takes time; I *need* time. I don't want to be somebody's kid my whole life. It's not that I don't like him ["that much," I almost added], it's just that the timing is bad. I mean, even if things were normal, right now is when I want to start having my *own* life. Is that too much to ask?"

I found I was getting mad at *her* now, and realized that wasn't going to help. So I tried to reassure her that everything was going to be all right. That I would go out more on the weekends with him and the twins when he came and that I'd try to fix things up as best I could.

"I was even thinking of asking him to help me learn to drive," I said.

I am *constantly* amazed at the things that come out of my mouth. If I was ever in the army, I'd tell them right off never to tell me the passwords to the Pentagon computers; I'd blab them to the first spy I'd meet.

"I don't want you to do anything that you wouldn't want to," said my mom. "I'm just feeling kind of blue, I guess. I don't think he'll go through with it."

So put it all down to love for a woman that I'm here behind the wheel of the middle-age-crisis-mobile, learning to drive from my father, after all. So, OK, the woman happens to be my mom.

For his part, I have to give him credit, Dad warmed up to the idea right away.

"Sure, son," he said. "Sure, I'd be happy to."

Note that this is also the first time he ever called me "son." I don't know what to make of this. Maybe he's been reading books or seeing a counselor.

Oh, and also note that the car I am (attempting) to drive is a stick shift. Oh, and if that isn't enough, did I mention that it's some soup-can English car, with the steering wheel on the wrong side?

My dad is the last of the warm-blooded mammals

that think a stick shift is really standard equipment on a car. "*You* decide when to shift, not some box stuffed with gears," is his mantra on this. Also, if you have engine problems, you can nurse it along longer before they try to rip you off for a tune-up, and also something about the snow when you can put it in a higher or lower gear (I forget which) and get more traction. He would also love it if cars still had a hand choke, although the last one he had, he fouled the plugs so bad they had to be replaced every six months. All of which is based on driving an army-surplus World War II jeep that somebody *gave* my grandfather once (so you know it was good) and who then taught my father everything he knows. The extra added attraction to English cars was also something left over from World War II, when my grandfather served over in England. Some GIs brought back unexploded shells and wrecked their neighborhoods; he brought back a taste for English cars, and polluted the family's automotive pool.

And here on the very first day of my very first lesson is what my dad starts with: "OK, now, Colm—son—I want you to concentrate now on what I'm telling you. Before you start the car, you push down on the clutch pedal. OK? And turn the ignition key and let it kick over, then give it a little gas. Then you shift into first—see here's the pattern on the knob—and let up *slooowly* on the clutch pedal until you feel it start to catch. Then you feed it a little more gas until it's caught all the way, so it doesn't stall out, and it gets moving, and then keep accelerating until you reach fifteen hundred rpms—watch it on the tach—then press down on the clutch pedal again—let off on the gas a little so you don't race the engine, and put it into second, and all the way up through the gears. Got it?"

You have to say "Yes" or he's already getting mad—he hates repeating himself. And you don't want to get off on the wrong foot—whichever one that is. I figure it'll come to me as I go along, anyway.

Well, all I can say is that I see why cars today have headrests. By the end of my first lesson, our heads were whipped around so much they were dangling by what must have been only single tendons.

The first time I tried, I forgot to shift. I knew something was wrong when I had the clutch pedal all the way up and the engine running fast up near where the red line is on the tach, and we weren't going anywhere. To give him credit, Dad didn't say a thing. I wasn't used to this kind of thick silence from him, though, and it only made it worse, since I could hear in my own mind the twenty things he was thinking.

"OK, Colm," he said calmly. "You probably know what you did wrong. Now try again."

Next shot, I remembered to put it in gear, but left rubber—about a quarter inch of it, anyway—before we stalled out. Next, I got us going, but off the side of the road, since I wasn't paying that close attention to steering.

And then there was the stop sign.

I have to admit right here, right up front, that my idea of driving was a little dysfunctional. From watching everyone, including my dad, I thought the secret was to drive like you had to pee real bad and the nearest bathroom was across the state. So when it came to a stop sign, I just did what I saw everybody else do. Slow down and take a look, keep it in gear, keep it rolling, save all that pedal hip-hop.

This is when Dad finally said something.

"Stop means *stop*," he said. "You've got to obey the laws."

This seemed obvious, and I thought I did stop anyway, but I didn't say anything, since I knew he would consider it backtalk.

After a while, he had me stop and practice getting it into first and moving and stopping. ("You press down the clutch pedal and put the shift in neutral and let up on the clutch and—this is very important—put your clutch foot on the floor. *Then* step on the brake.") Driving it seemed wasn't the fun it looked like at all, but a tricky series of movements you had to follow as closely as if you were dismantling a bomb.

"You changed lanes without looking."

"I looked in the mirror like you said."

"You could fit a truck into what you can't see in the

mirror," he said. "Turn your head like this [Here he helpfully twisted my head and popped a few neck vertebrae] and *look*."

And after an hour or so of this I'd had it for the day.

I think he had, too, since when I suggested we go back and have lunch, he agreed pretty quickly. He wanted to take us all out for lunch then, Mom included, and so we all went—Mom and Dad up front, me squeezed in the little jump seat back among the kidlings again. Mom wore what she calls her Sunday smile the whole time, even when Dad forgot what she took in her coffee. And later when he said we should all go out to watch them fly model planes out at the old airstrip, she said she wasn't feeling well and wanted to go home, so we dropped her off.

I wanted to keep her company, but wanted to keep her happy by spending time with Dad, too, so I didn't know *what* to do, but she said, "I really need to rest. Colm, you go with your father," and that settled it.

It was kind of fun to watch the planes, anyway. Some were real big, although they looked pretty small once they got up there, and one guy even had a helicopter. The twins loved it, and we stopped by a roadside stand and got them ice cream before he brought us home.

I tiptoed into the house and tried to keep the twins quiet, but they got in a fight about whose turn it was to feed Spike, their hamster, and next they were yelling. My mom came out of her bedroom all bleary-eyed but smiling and hugged them to her, even while they were struggling to get at each other.

"Good show!" said Marlene when I told her what had happened with my dad and the driving lesson.

"This might work," I said. "He seems a little different."

"And you?" she said.

"I can fake it. For a while, anyway."

I was helping her fix the canoe. She'd hit an old snag in the lake, and it ripped the canvas covering on an area the size of a dinner plate. She got a piece of matching canvas for a patch and was kneeling next to a camp stove in her yard stirring a can of reeking glue.

"Where'd you learn all this?" I asked.

"My dad," she said.

"You don't seem to have the same problems with him like I do with mine," I said.

"From everything you tell me, my dad seems to have more patience," she admitted. "I watched him once fix the motor on that washing machine. He could've bought another one, or even got a used motor at the junkyard, but he took the old motor apart and rewound the wire on it and got it working again."

She stopped stirring the glue and looked up at me.

"Do you know how much wire there is in an electric motor?" she said.

I said I didn't.

"Lots," she said. "It must've been a mile. And he wound up every bit of it. Good and tight and neat. Took him days. Made a little spinning jig specially to do it. Said he didn't want to waste all that perfectly good metal and that he'd appreciate it better that way."

"My dad would've thrown the whole washer out, and got a new one," I said. "What makes people different like that I wonder?" I said. "Here, let me hold that steady for you."

She was smearing the patch canvas with the glue and it was moving around on the scrap of plywood she had it on.

"You'd better use those," she said, nodding toward a couple of sticks on the ground nearby. "You get any of this stuff on you, and you'll be a permanent part of my canoe."

She worked quickly and quietly for a few minutes.

"My dad was probably poor as yours, from what you told me," she said after a while, "but he seemed to ride it out much better. He pretty much stayed in one place—a farm—the whole time he was growing up. His mom had lived in the city, and *his* dad had a heart attack and died, and she had the idea, my grandma this is, that the only way she was going to keep them all together and fed was to work a farm, so she took the insurance money and bought one. She was from the city and had no clue how to work it, but she was so determined that the farmer who sold her the land showed her some things, and she got the local banker to lend her the money to plant, and she made something of it, and it actually did work out for them. There."

She finished coating the piece of canvas, expertly laid it over the torn area on the canoe surface, and began smoothing it. I noticed her hands as she worked the stiff fabric: They were deeply tanned but not rough-looking. Her nails, which were painted with a clear, shiny polish, ended in smooth, natural curves that wouldn't get in the way if you found you had to do a little work, like patching a canoe, for instance. She was working air bubbles out from under the patch and I tried to help her, but as soon as I chased one to the edge, another formed behind it.

"Here, use your palms. Let me show you," she said, and put both of her smaller hands on top of mine, and guided them, so the little bubbles got all corraled up and herded out. She leaned toward me as she was doing this and I wasn't trying, I swear, but I could see down to where the third button on her pullover was open. There was definitely some news from that country since last summer.

"Hey, watch," she said, as I went off the edge and got some of the glue on my hands.

"I *was*," I said.

"Yeah, but what," she said, tossing me a rag and blushing as she fixed the last button.

I smiled as I wiped my hands.

"That should do it," she said, patting the canoe.

Rule 6: Different people are different.

Seven

Next Friday, I was sitting out on the front steps lining up the sights on my BB gun at a soda can across the street, when I caught some movement out of the corner of my eye. It was Carmella, live and in person. She wasn't supposed to come out until the next day, but there she was—tanned and gorgeous in her short shorts, white blouse tied up above her midriff, a big straw bag over her shoulder.

"Come swimming with me," she said. It was part command, part promise, and no part question. I quickly put down the gun. Plinking cans seemed like such a kid thing to be doing. I was speechless.

"You OK?" she said, looking a little worried.

"Sure," I said. "I mean, OK, I'd really like to go with you," and I ran in and got suited up.

I told my mom where I was going and took a quick check in the mirror. One thing, at least with all the swimming, my build wasn't so bad. Although I'd lost a little since I quit over the winter, definition was coming back nice with all the work I was getting in.

"Let's see that Dean guy get pumped like this from spinning a steering wheel," I thought, throwing a towel around my neck.

It was one of those perfect days you get in early summer: not too hot or too cool, a sky made bluer by one bright, backlit cloud, and just enough breeze to push a few strands of hair across Carmella's face where they caught in the corners of her mouth and she slowly drew them out, all wet on the ends. As we walked—it was only a couple of blocks along the lake to the beach—she saw something out in the water—it looked like a heron—and got real close next to me and pointed so I breathed in her perfume.

The beach was deserted. Too early in the morning for anyone to be there except for a few kids and a bored lifeguard who didn't do much guarding for the time it took Carmella to wriggle out of her tight shorts. Underneath, she had on a two-piece, wider than a lot of girls were wearing that year, something her mother probably "helped" her to pick out, and when she took off the blouse, you could see she was still not as tanned on her stomach.

She no sooner kicked her sandals off than she was running. I followed close behind. She dove, expertly slicing into the water, and with quiet strokes was out at the raft in a minute or two. She pulled herself up on it in one smooth move, and when I tried to get up, she laughed and pushed me back in with her foot. I dove under and came up on the other side of the raft and quickly pulled myself up before she could get me, and tried to wrestle her in, but she was strong and when I shoved harder, she stepped aside and I went flying in.

"Truce. Truce," she said as I grabbed the side of the raft. She put out a hand to help me up, but let go and I fell in again. Next time I grabbed the side and shot myself up out of the water and onto the raft, landing so hard on my stomach that I was winded for a few seconds and lay there like a fish pulled into a boat.

"Colm?" she said, worried, touching my back with the tips of her fingers. I had the taste of tin you get in your mouth when you've gotten a good wallop, but I swallowed it down, and said, "I'm fine."

Fortunately, she lay down next to me so I didn't have to try standing up. It was much warmer out on the raft, and we lay side by side like this in the sun for a while, drying off. She told me about her first couple of weeks working the office job in the city—her first real job after baby-sitting. On her first day of work, an old metal wastebasket had started smoking, right there in the middle of the office, and nobody seemed to notice, so she tried to ignore it too, even though it was right near her desk. Finally, it triggered off the smoke alarm and someone put a fire extinguisher to it.

When they asked her why she didn't say anything, she said, "I thought that's what you did with your trash." Everyone laughed and she felt embarrassed. "But how would I know? No one told me," she said.

It did sound kind of dumb, but maybe I would've done the same. Who knows? It was like everything else: How do you *really* know until it happens to you?

"It's hard to figure out what's the right thing to do all the time," I said.

Suddenly, Carmella raised up on an elbow and looked at something on my other side, and I turned to see the familiar, old, beat-up canoe bearing down on us, Marlene leisurely paddling from its stern. What was *she* doing here? I lay back down like I didn't see her. She came right up to the raft, bumping the canoe into it.

"Hi, Colm. Carmella," she said. "Hi," I said, putting up an arm, but not sitting up. I put the arm over my eyes as if to cover them from the sun. "Long time . . ." This to Carmella. "What're you guys doing out here so early, anyways?"

I mumbled something about "hanging out," then realized what a double meaning it had and got all embarrassed. I felt awkward like I was caught at something I shouldn't be doing. But what? Carmella was very gracious, though, and she and Marlene talked a little while about what they'd done the year before and then Marlene said to me: "Colm, you practicing lately? You haven't been out."

"Practicing for what?" Carmella asked me.

"Colm's trying to swim the lake," said Marlene, beaming like I was her little brother or something.

"Across the *whole* lake?" said Carmella with a little too much show.

"I don't know," I said. "It's something to do."

"You must be a good swimmer, being on the team and all," she said, looking more closely, I imagined, at my arms and chest.

"He quit this year, though," said Marlene.

"You quit?" said Carmella.

"Well, I *was* on almost all season this year, and since grade school, but I'm not anymore, like Marlene says." I didn't want to get into why, and fortunately Carmella didn't seem curious to know.

"But you *are* swimming the lake?"

"I got nearly halfway last time," I said.

"I'd like to *watch* you sometime." Carmella said this like she was saying she wanted to see me get naked.

"I always go out with Colm—to spot him," Marlene put in. "You could come, too, if you want."

"No," said Carmella, "that's all right. I wouldn't want to interfere." Like Marlene and I were engaged or something.

"It's no interference," said Marlene, not picking up on where Carmella was coming from.

"I don't know if I need anyone to go along anymore, anyway," I said to Marlene, looking at her for the first time since she came up.

She gave me a funny look. "But what if you get in trouble?"

"I'm getting pretty far already without any trouble. I think I can handle it," I said.

Marlene frowned, then something seemed to click and she suddenly said, "Gotta go. You guys have fun," and shoved off.

" 'Bye," said Carmella.

I couldn't think of anything right to say after this, and Carmella said nothing. I peeked out of the side of my eyes at her and she was lying there with her eyes open, staring at the sky. Then she stood up. "Let's go in," she said. "It's getting a little too chilly out here," and she dove in and swam for shore.

I went in after her, not feeling so good all of a sudden. When we got back on the beach, Carmella buried her head in a movie magazine and I lay on my stomach, playing with the sand.

I only shot a brief glance out on the lake once or twice the rest of the time we were on the beach, but

Marlene must've paddled in or something, 'cause I didn't see her out there. The lake looked empty without her.

"Did I tell you I was learning to drive?" I said—a desperate bit, one I'd been saving as a surprise to tell Carmella when I nearly had the license and when I was sure it would all work out.

"You are?" she said, suddenly all alert, her magazine put down. "When do you get your license?"

"I hope in the next month—before the end of August, anyway. I need to take the test and everything."

"That's great!" she said. "August is the best up at Barstow." And she rolled over and gave me a kiss, on the lips—long and sweet and wet.

That weekend, my father was in some kind of mood. His one-man-all-American-good-guy show looked like it was coming to the end of its run. Maybe it was because he and Mom weren't talking; maybe he had a putrid week, I don't know. But his patience was as thin as the hair on top of his head, which he kept running his hands over during the whole driving lesson, plastering it to his skull.

And so when I hit a pothole hard, he shouted, "Didn't you see that?"

"Yeah," I said, "I tried to go *over* it. I thought if I went fast enough . . ."

"What do you think this is?" he said. "A movie? This thing doesn't *fly*, damn it!" he said. "I hope you didn't break something." And he made me pull over so he could make a show of huffing around and looking under the car as if he could tell about anything beyond a flat, which fortunately we didn't have.

And if that wasn't good enough, he picked that weekend to try to teach me parallel parking. We used some old, rusted fifty-gallon barrels that were in a parking lot near the lake. A bait shop was there when I was a kid and I remember Dad getting mad at me because I didn't want to touch the nasty-looking sandworms he bought to take us fishing. The place was gone now, burned and bulldozed over, but the lot was still there. Dad got out and rolled a couple of the barrels so they were about a car and a half length apart, and I was supposed to get the car parked between them.

"Dad," I said. "I really don't know if I'm ready for this."

He forced out another tiny dab of cheeriness, like that last sick gob of toothpaste you can get after you take the tube out of the trash basket and squeeze it till it bleeds?

"Don't underestimate yourself, now, Colm. Let's give it a try, anyway, son," he said.

Then he gave me a five-minute (I timed it on the dashboard clock) detailed explanation of how to go about it, from the beginning precise "entry angle" (in degrees) to the final "front and rear check," complete with all the shiftings and clutchings and brakings and wheel turnings so it sounded like I was docking a space shuttle.

This time, I didn't even pretend like I got it.

I pulled up next to the front barrel.

"Too close! Too close!" he barked. "Watch you don't scrape the car. What did I tell you? Leave some air space."

So next time I pulled up too wide.

Then I got it right, but blew it by cutting in too sharp.

Then I got in, but hit the rear barrel, and it took me five maneuvers and sweating and turning and clutching to get it straightened out.

"Again," said my dad.

And I tried it again, this time coming in too shallow.

"Again." You could see his ears going way red now.

It was like the car and barrels were those little magnetic dogs? First the barrels pulled me in and I couldn't get far enough away, and then I couldn't get close enough. None of this was helped, of course, by having to be all the while furiously pushing down pedals and shifting and turning the wheel and looking over my shoulder. I felt like one of those guys you see on TV, juggling a bowling ball and a machete and a blowtorch.

Finally, I gave it too much gas once, missed the barrels entirely, and backed it through one of the rotted logs that were supposed to stop you from driving into the lake.

"The other way! Put it in first; we're sliding down!" But it wouldn't go into first, and I raced the engine in neutral. "Stop! Stop!" Dad yelled as the car started to slide down the bank and he jerked up on the emergency brake between us, exactly as I managed to get it into first, so that the car lurched forward and stalled.

We sat there quiet for a few minutes, the car pointed up so you could see underneath the branches of the trees, my dad with his hand over his face.

"Put it in first," he said after a while. So I did.

"Push down on the clutch pedal." I did this.

"Turn on the ignition." The engine roared to life—overaccelerated.

"Easy," he said. "Let up on the clutch." I felt the car strain against the brake. He released it and we crept forward. Luckily the ground was firm and I was able to get the car up in the lot.

"Let's go," my father said. "That's enough for one day."

We rode in silence for a while. Except, you know how your stomach makes noises after you've eaten a big meal? Well, I could almost hear his brain gurgling with all he wanted to say.

"I don't know if this is going to work," he finally said in a low, matter-of-fact voice. "You simply don't listen. You don't do anything the way I tell you."

"Dad," I said, "it's one thing to tell someone something and another to actually *do* it."

"Don't get wise on me," he said. Wisdom being one of the cardinal sins in the catechism of coaching.

"Dad," I said, frustrated, "that's the first time ever that I even *tried* to park. Give me a little room to make a few mistakes, will you?" and right when I said this, a kid shot out of a drive ahead of us on a skateboard; not looking—probably like I did a hundred times when I was his age—the only thing different being he was about to be a bug on our windshield.

Q: What's the last thing that goes through a skateboarder's mind when he hits your windshield?

A: His skateboard.

"The brake!" my father shouted, but I must've hit the clutch pedal instead, since I had that sort of weightless feeling you get when you tense up for the Gs but nothing happens. My dad lunged over and hit the horn and the kid tipped up on the sidewalk, and flipped his skateboard and middle finger before taking off.

"That does it," my dad said. "I give up. Get out of

there. Let me drive."

I stopped the car and got out. I saw he was going

around front and I went that way too. I swear I was going to give him a shove. But we passed each other without bloodshed, got back in the car, and drove off.

The obedient son, once again taking his licks.

Rule 7: "Mistakes" is the name we give to our experiences.

Eight

Uncle Junior took the dowsing rod down from the gun rack in the back window of the Hog. This was one of the ways he sold people on hiring him: Instead of having to get a water witcher to find where to drill like most people out here in the country, and someone else to do the drilling, he'd do both. He'd save the customer time and money and guarantee the result, "all in one, neat, brown-paper-wrapped package," as he told the farmer we were working for. The farmer was a guy about as old as my father. He was wearing a suit and tie and high rubber boots when he met us.

"Going to see my broker." He sounded like he was apologizing for the weird outfit. He showed us the general area where he was thinking of putting the well—the original was under the house and the new site was slightly up the hill from it—and then he went off to one of the barns.

Uncle Junior started working the area with the rod, holding one fork in the same hand he held the crutch handle and the other in his free hand. It jerked and bobbled with every step like the end of a downed electric wire. The farmer came out of the barn and watched this show for a few minutes before hosing down his boots, peeling them off, and putting on a pair of leather ones. Then he got into his pickup and took off. When he was out of sight, Uncle Junior sat on a freshly cut tree stump, pulled a cigarette out of his shirt pocket, and took a drag.

"How's it coming?" I said. "You getting any pulls?"

"Not yet."

"How do you know when you hit something, anyway?" I asked him. "I mean, it looks like the thing is jerking around all the time. How do you know when it's real?"

"You just know," said Uncle Junior. "Don't ask me how." He smiled and threw the cigarette butt into the soft dirt.

He continued limping back and forth across the field, the dowsing rod in front of him like the hitch to some invisible team of horses. Suddenly the stick seemed to take an extra specially deep dive and Uncle Junior leaned forward as if it were pulling him. He called to me to put a few rocks in the spot, then hobbled back to the Hog to hang up the rod and begin setting up.

Later, while we ate lunch, I tried again: "I mean you really don't believe that little stick is going to somehow pick up water underground," I said. "It would pull over to the cistern there"—I pointed to the farmhouse—"long before it would point to water way down there"—I pointed to the otherwise unmarked ground where we had set up the rig.

"First off, it only goes for moving water," he said. Then he bit off and chewed a big piece of sandwich thoughtfully, and for so long, I thought he wasn't going to say anything else. Then he finally said: "Second, it's a good show. People like it when you give them a little more for their money, especially something they don't totally understand. It makes them think all the more you're an expert. And third, well, I could give you lots of other reasons, but Colm, what it really comes down to is this: How else am I really going to go about it?"

He took another bite, chewed it carefully, and swallowed before speaking again. "Look," he said. "Forget all the mysterioso crap. It's a practical thing. I could drill where we set up the rig there, or ten feet over, or a hundred, or right here where we're sitting. So let's say I happen to pick a spot—maybe I like it 'cause it's flat so I can set the Hog up easy. Then we get down eighty or ninety feet and ain't hit nothing yet.

"Now I got a decision to make: Do I keep throwing pipe in a dry hole, or do I reel in my line and try somewhere else? If somewhere else, where? If I'd picked any old spot, I'd as likely quit and cut bait, even though I still might have a good chance to get a strike. So what it *does* is gives me a starting place I have some faith in—somewhere to work from. You see?"

"Then you *don't* believe it really works?" I said.

He put his sandwich down on a paper napkin on the tailgate of the Hog and drew a cup of lemonade from the spigot of the big cooler he had sitting in the back. "No," he said, "it works *great.* It gives me a reason to keep going."

That seemed to make sense.

"How do you really *know,* though, when the thing really pulls down, and it's not only you pushing it?"

He suddenly looked weary like there was so much explaining to do, and life was so short. "Well, you don't," he said. "Not the way you know history or geometry or something in a book. It *feels* different, is all. You know when you're doing it right, when you're hitting the sweet spot. It's unconscious, like riding a bicycle or swimming or driving a car."

"Funny you should bring that up," I said, telling him what happened with my dad.

"Yeah, well, don't you see that was the problem," Uncle Junior said. "He was trying to *tell* you. Can't tell anybody anything. What you really need to do is to get your *own* feel for it."

"But how do you get that feel," I said, "without *doing* it?"

"You don't," said Junior. "It's like how do you learn to keep from falling out of bed at night? Now, don't get me wrong, telling can save time—get you there quicker—but it's no substitution for the real thing. So, in the end, Colm, a rod can show you where to dig, but you got to work the shovel. Come on, let's get back to work."

I wish I had a divining rod that could show *me* where to start.

We hit water on the second day at seventy feet—quick for wells around here—and, since Uncle Junior didn't have another job lined up right away, I found I had the rest of the week off. It was one of the worst weeks of the summer—any summer. I couldn't find a way to climb out of the deep well of blues I was thrashing around in.

Even Marlene wasn't out on the lake. I saw her once out at her station on the back porch "watching out," but when I called over to her, she just waved and went into the house. Who did I have to blame for this, treating her like I did the other day out at the raft, like she was someone trying to hit me up for pocket change? I'd pretty much given up on my swimming, anyway, except for some laps out to the raft in the morning, and I didn't even keep count with those.

The following week, Dad called late Friday afternoon saying there was some important contract he had to complete at the office and he couldn't come out that weekend. My mom tried to explain it to the kids, but couldn't get it to make sense in a way they could really understand. I mean, if he was a garbageman . . . But the twins wouldn't know a contract from a candy wrapper. Me, I might be able to tell it from an excuse, but I'm not positive. So she told them Dad was busy, and that he promised to come out next week for sure.

Maybe it was coincidence, but I couldn't help but feel this was his way of showing me he didn't need the trouble.

MEMO

TO: COLM
FROM: DAD
RE: DRIVING

- IF YOU'RE NOT GOING TO PERFORM TO MY STANDARDS, I DON'T NEED THE AGGRAVATION.
- REMEMBER WE HAVE SOME HISTORY IN THIS REGARD INVOLVING YOUR SWIMMING.
- I HAVE A LIFE OF MY OWN NOW.

I also felt that I let my mom down. Even though she didn't say anything—she *wouldn't* anyway—I could see she was in an even deeper well than me.

I thought I'd give her a break on Saturday. I saw Dean's car at Carmella's and there was no way I was going down there, so I told Mom I'd take the twins to the beach, so she could have a little time for herself. A woman she knew down the block was driving to the mall a couple of towns over, and maybe they could take in a movie and do some shopping or something. So I threw all the twins' junk in a plastic bag, and led them down the road to the beach.

I knew it was a mistake for me to be there as soon as I saw Dean's car parked outside the gates to the beach. They must've driven down in the time it took for me to get the twins and all their stuff together. It was only a couple of blocks from Carmella's to there, but he'd probably drive if he was going across the street to pick up a quarter he dropped. I could see Carmella and Dean out on the raft. I thought maybe I could convince the twins to leave, but they whooped and leaped into the water before I could even set the bag down, and soon were into some serious sand play, and I knew it would take heavy equipment and a lot of noise to pull them out of there. After a while I got into it myself, and let them bury their big brother in the sand. I had them put a big hat on me so maybe Carmella and Dean wouldn't see. When I was pretty much buried, with only my head sticking out, Carmella and Dean came in. "Hey, kids," said Carmella, who recognized the twins right away, then saw me—a big mound of sand with a straw hat on one end. "Colm!" she said.

"Hi," said Dean, without much enthusiasm.

I mumbled "Hello," and tried to get up, but the twins wouldn't have it, and started screaming, pushing me back down.

"Colm, don't mess up all the twins' hard work," said Carmella, and she knelt down to help them fix the damage. Dean stayed standing with his arms folded, looking back at the parking lot, probably checking out his car to make sure some fly hadn't taken a dump on it.

Carmella worked away, getting all sweaty, her breasts in line with my head. "There," she said when they were done, but then Robbie had to knock off the hat and put his sand pail on my head.

Carmella laughed. "It's a little small for you," she said.

I smiled, feeling *really* stupid.

"Dean, check this out," she said.

He looked and smiled. Something suddenly seemed to come to him.

"Hey, how's it going with swimming the lake?" he said. It was more like a challenge than a question. "Carmella tells me you're trying to swim across." Heavy on the "trying."

"Yeah," I said. "I'm working on it."

"I mean, it must be a couple of miles," he said.

"I'm on the swim team," I said.

"I thought you quit?" said Carmella.

Then I remembered telling her out at the raft that day. "Yeah, well, just this year," I said to Dean. "But I've been practicing almost every day."

"I guess you got to do something with yourself all week," he said. The way he said it, you could take it two ways. I'm sure he meant it the second.

"I keep pretty busy," I said.

Dean looked back at his car and nudged Carmella with his elbow.

"I'm working on my driver's license, too," I added.

"But Uncle Junior said you had a fight with your dad," said Carmella. It was hard to say anything without halfway taking it back, it seemed. Carmella must have been checking up on me, asking questions. Uncle Junior would have never told her on his own. I should be flattered, I guess, that she asked about me. But I also felt like she was thinking I was a liar.

"That was last week," I said. "We had some words is all. I'm planning on getting back to it when he comes out again."

"Had my license two years now," said Dean.

"Where Dean was from, you could get your license early," said Carmella.

Where was that? Soybean-sucking country where they throw kids out in the field at five years old to ride a tractor barefoot? I thought of asking. But I didn't.

"Well, give me a call next week," she said, tapping on the top of the pail with her long, red fingernails.

"See ya," said Dean, and he put his arm around her waist as they walked past me up the beach. Buried as I was, I couldn't really turn around, but after a few minutes I heard the showy roar of Dean's car. I'm sure if he could have worked it, he would have sprayed sand on me as he peeled out.

I was kind of pissed at Uncle Junior. I guess I didn't say he should keep quiet about me quitting the driving lessons with my dad, but why would he tell *her* about it? Was he trying to screw things up between me and her, or what?

Early one morning at the end of the week, my mom came up to the attic to get me. On cooler days I hid out up there so I could have some sort of place to call my own.

"Junior is here. He's got something to show you," she said from the stairs.

Uncle Junior was out front in his Buick, his hair all slicked back and looking like he'd already been up for hours.

"What's up?" I said. "You got another job for me?"

"Come on," he said. "Get in."

We drove down to the big shed where he kept the Hog.

I got out and he hobbled along ahead of me, and shoved aside the heavy sliding door.

"Check it out," he said.

The Hog sat there. At first, it looked no different than before. Then the light caught on some reflective metal below the front bumper: a license plate!

"What's going on?" I asked.

"Get in," he said.

I climbed up in the high driver's seat, all bare springs with a piece of plywood wired on top to sit on.

"Turn it over," he said.

I jiggled the stick to make sure it was in neutral, then turned the key, bracing for the blast. But instead of spitting flames, the thing positively hummed.

"What's going on?" I said. "You fixed it?"

"She's all street legal. Only had to rig some taillights and get a junk converter and muffler. Save me from towing it everywhere, anyways. It's getting too tough on the Buick. Thought you might like to try her out."

"Me?" I said.

"Yeah, I heard you can drive good enough as long as there ain't any barrels in your way."

He got up in the seat beside me.

It took a little getting used to, everything being on the other side—where it's *supposed* to be, by the way—

and the clutch felt different, too—it cut in a little higher up—but I got it all under control pretty quick.

"Come on," said Uncle Junior, "let's take her out."

I eased the clutch into first. It bucked and stalled. Uncle Junior was looking out the side window at something, and didn't seem to notice. I got it started again and began to crawl forward. The brakes were tighter than I thought they'd be, and I made a jerky stop at the end of the drive, but then got it off smoothly in first, and out onto the road.

"Let her go," said Junior, after I'd shifted up to top gear, and I pushed down on the accelerator to feel the Hog lurch ahead with a sudden spurt of power.

"Wow," I said, "what else did you do to this?"

"Couple of things I picked up from modifying old cars."

We drove around a little. I only got nervous when we were out in traffic around the lake, and aside from once forgetting to put on a turn signal, I didn't screw up much at all.

When we got back, I felt like I was vibrating all over—maybe from the bad suspension. "When you fix an old car, you gotta stop somewhere," he said.

"Thanks," I said, "that was fun."

"Practice again tomorrow, early?" he asked. "I'm going to need somebody who can drive this thing, you know."

"Sure," I said.

"Give you a lift?" said Uncle Junior.

"No, I'll walk it."

And when I got home, I was so excited, my mother had to remind me to eat lunch.

Rule 8: If you're stuck in a well, feel around for the rope.

Nine

I expected my driving test to be a lot tougher. Nearly aced the written part. Only missed the one on what you're supposed to do in a high wind.

Answer: Slow down and pull over to the side of the road.

I should have guessed: Alien invasion? Meteor strike? Wall of hot lava bearing down on your vehicle?

Slow down and pull over to the side of the road. Membership in Mensa not required.

The actual road test was a little shakier, however. In our state, you get a highway patrolman—Smokey Bear hat and all—to sit next to you with a clipboard and pen.
What I try to do when I'm in scary situations like this, is talk; it calms me down a little when the others talk

back. Shows me they're human, too, I guess. The guy I pulled, though, failed Humanity 101. Hadn't had a laugh since he snapped jockstraps back in his high school locker room. I tried: "Must have some interesting things happen in this job?"

"Nope," he said.

"My first time at this, but I've practiced a lot."

"Yup."

"You have to get special training for this?"

"Just drive, please, son."

I'm sure I could learn to hate being called "son."

But I performed flawlessly—well, nearly so, anyway. My only mistake? "You signaled too soon before coming to a turn." Maybe putting on the signal a block ahead of time *was* a little early, but I wanted no surprises for my fellow drivers.

Of course, I had a great teacher. Even with the limits of the Hog, Uncle Junior was so patient, dragging quietly on his cigarette, giving a word or two of reinforcement, allowing me to make nonfatal mistakes, which I would quickly realize, or he would gently announce. Asking me to rate myself after each trip and tell him where I could have done better before he made his own "suggestions," as he called them. I took more ownership of the thing. Didn't feel like I was being manipulated like one of those model airplanes with a radio control box. Wasn't long before Uncle Junior said: "You're wasting my time with this. Go take the test."

And so I did.

My mom sprung for a rental car. Uncle Junior had a shoebusting time of it trying to find me one with a stick so I wouldn't be thrown too far off. We had to leave the rental agency with Uncle Junior in the driver's seat, faking it for a few blocks, crossing over to the pedals with his good leg. Then I drove it, up until a block or so before we got to the old shopping mall where they had the driving test, then Uncle Junior got behind the wheel again. At least he knew enough not to talk up Dudley Don'tblab. And I breezed through it. Biggest anticlimax of my life next to growing hair in my pits.

"Colm has something he wants to celebrate," my mom told my dad next time he came out. We had grudgingly begun talking again—as long as it had nothing to do with the car, or driving, or swimming, or life in general—so I flinched a little when she said this. My dad got that hunted look he had like when he forgot their anniversary or something.

"Your birthday is September, right, Colm?" he said.

"October," I said.

"Show him," said Mom, feeling sorry for the old guy.

I pulled out my wallet—which up to this point had all of two dollars and a picture of some babe they put in at the wallet factory—took out the license, and handed it to him.

"When did you . . . ?" he started to say.

"You gave me a real good start at it, Dad," I said. "More than you think. It took a little time to sink in, is all. Uncle Junior worked with me a little driving the Hog, I took the test, and that was it."

"The Hog?" he said.

I explained about Uncle Junior's well-drilling rig.

"Great!" he said, all the columns finally adding up. He seemed to be truly happy for me.

"Yes," he said. "This does indeed demand a celebration. Where should we go?"

He asked this last of Mom, who at first didn't seem to hear him. Then she realized he was talking to *her*.

"You want *me* to pick it out?" she said.

"Why not?" said Dad. Was the old control freak finally learning to let go of the wires a little?

Afterward, I couldn't wait to get in touch with Carmella, to tell *her* the good news, but she didn't come out that weekend. When I dialed her number in the city, which I dragged out of Uncle Junior, I got what must've been her aunt. She didn't speak English real well, and I didn't know if Carmella got the message.

But then the first thing next Saturday morning, she called.

"Colm!" she said. "This is fabulous. When do we go?"

I was ready for this, too.

"Well, that's the next hurdle," I said. "I have to get my dad's car. He's supposed to be out later," I said.

"You haven't asked him yet?" she said.

"He's just getting used to the idea that I got a driver's license without him punching the buttons on the control box," I said. "I've got to give him a little time."

"So, after lunch?"

"Well, not exactly," I said. "I need to talk with him about it. Maybe not until tomorrow."

There was a silence at the other end of the line.

"But The Shores doesn't open until after noon on Sunday," she said.

I didn't know what to say.

"I'll work on him," I said.

"OK," said Carmella. "Give me a call back when you've got it."

In other words: Forget about calling me *until* you've got it. She acted like I'd spit a piece of gum in her milk shake, but what could I do? Getting the car would be a real big step, given all Dad had wrapped up in both it and me. I thought my best way into all this would be through Mom. After all, she knew Dad best. I asked her, but she was already way ahead.

"I've got it all figured," she said.

And that day, I noticed little differences in the way she talked with him.

First of all, she did—talk with him, that is. It was all pretty natural since our little trip the week before to celebrate me getting my license, all squeezed together in Dad's tiny car. Mom had picked a big, noisy pizza place and we had a great time. Even when Robbie dumped his root beer in the middle of a pepperoni pizza, Dad hardly flinched.

So this time, when he showed up on Saturday morning, instead of rushing him off with the twins, she had him in for coffee. Then he took the twins out for the day, like normal, and, although I was still a little uncomfortable with it, I went along, too. More mending fences.

We went swimming, and this time, he actually got in the water with us. I mean, he swam the other times, but usually at the end after the kids were back on the blanket, he'd go out and do a couple of power laps. But this time, he put Robbie on his back, and I got Marie on mine and we had chicken fights, and he pulled the kids through the water. And when we got back all tired and sandy, my mom suggested he shower there. Mom found some of his old clothes still in the closet from last summer for him to change into. The pants were big around the waist, and they had a good laugh about it.

"Missing your good cooking," he said.

"Why not have dinner with us, then?" she said.

"Here?" he said. He seemed to think about it for a few seconds. "Why not?"

Dinner was great. My mom had been experimenting with her cooking since my dad left, and she served one of the new recipes—something with lots of fresh vegetables and noodles. The kids only ate the noodles, and my dad gave it a wary glance, but then he got into it and, with a glass of wine and some crisp bread from the local bakery, seemed to really enjoy it. I couldn't believe Mom could get away with serving him a meatless dinner in bold violation of the Prime Cut Directive. But then she was starting to get her own ideas about how to do things, and he *did* have a burger at the beach. And the stuff Mom made *was* really good. And it was in the glow after dinner and after the kids were in bed that Mom popped the Big Question.

We were watching some dumb black-and-white movie on TV. My parents had this great habit of talking during a movie, telling each other the obvious:

"She's picking up here that he loves her, but she doesn't want to show *she* loves *him*."

"The guy in the hat. He's got a gun. He's going to shoot them!"

"She's going to stow away on the boat now. She won't let him go like that."

Closed captioning for the brain-dead. Just like the old days.

Finally the thing was over.

"The End," said my mother.

"MCMXXXIV," said my father. "That's nineteen thirty-four."

"Frank, let Colm use the car tomorrow," said my mother.

"OK," said my dad. "I was wondering when he was going to ask."

Soon after this, I said good night and went to bed. I could hear my dad say, "Good night, Rebecca," and then heard his car start up, and my mother's bedroom door close. Well, what did you expect? So they *didn't* sleep together that night. Walking on water wasn't built in a day.

I could hardly get any sleep myself, and next morning, I was up with the sun. I didn't want to call Carmella so early, so I got my coffee and banana and went out on the back steps. The sky was overcast; maybe it would rain later, and cool down. I was starting to have enough summer, anyway, but I hoped the rain would hold off at least until Carmella and I got back from Barstow.

I caught a glimpse of Marlene, paddling off into the gray lake in her canoe. I wanted to call after her, but she was already too far out. Then I suddenly remembered the dream I was having right before I woke. I was out in the canoe, but it was with Carmella instead, although I knew there was something not quite right about this. As I put my paddle in the water, I noticed there was someone down there—underwater. It was a guy—he looked like me. He was sitting there on the bottom, his skin looking all yellow from the color of the water. His lips were moving like he was trying to say something, but nothing was coming out. I turned to tell Carmella that we should do something to help him. "We don't have time," she said. But you could tell it was something else—she was afraid of breaking a fingernail or something. So we went on and it was with those feelings—something missed I should have done—that I woke up.

I waited until ten, and called.

"What? Who is this?" Aunt Tessie answered. "Colm? Carmella's at church. I'll tell her to call you when she gets back, OK?"

"OK," I said.

Another couple hours of hanging.

"You got it?"

It's Carmella on the phone. How does she know it's me picking up when it rings? Does she think I'm sitting here waiting, working my whole life around her? How come she's right?

"Yeah," I say. "I got it."

"What time?"

"Soon as you're ready," I say.

"Give me a half hour," she says. "I just got back from church."

A half hour later, to the minute, I'm out in front of her house. I park behind the convoy, and bound up the stairs.

"She says she'll be a few minutes." It's Tessie, one of the other matriarchs of the kitchen.

"Here, sit," she says. "You want something?"

"No, thanks," I say. I'm really too excited to eat.

"Some bread? A little sausage?" She's a little more aggressive than Louisa.

"No, that's OK," I say.

She's about to threaten me with more of the menu, when Carmella shows in long white slacks and big white cotton man's shirt, sun hat, and big straw bag.

" 'Bye, Auntie." She pecks Tessie on the cheek. "Let's go."

And I'm ahead of her, opening the door and out to the little green car.

She stops when she gets to it, a look of dismay on her face.

"*This* is your car?" she says.

"My father's, yeah," I say.

"It's so . . . little," she says.

"Yeah, well . . ." I don't know what to say. Of course it is. That's part of the thing.

"It's fun," I say. "Come on, get in."

She goes to get in the usual passenger side, and I have to stop her. Tell her about the English deal.

"I knew they *drove* on the wrong side of the road," she said, "but I didn't know they had the steering wheel and everything on the wrong side, too. This is too weird." She suddenly looked like she wasn't so sure of the whole thing.

Damn my father and the car he rode in on.

"This is strange, sitting over here," she said, as we took the familiar roads to Barstow.

"You should try *driving* it," I said.

Then I told her the whole story of my driving lessons, leaning on what I thought were the funny parts about trying to go airborne over the pothole and nearly backing into the lake.

"I didn't think it was that hard," she said. I tried to hear her saying she was amazed at how hard it was, but it kept sounding like I was someone who would need help using a pencil sharpener. I grinned my big dog grin, which left me open to all possibilities.

We were on the road only a few minutes when she popped the snap on her pants, squirmed out of them, and threw them in the tiny backseat, so she wore only her swimsuit bottom. She also unbuttoned the bottom buttons of the shirt and tied the tails up under her breasts. The top buttons were already open. "I can't take the shirt off," she said. "I don't have anything on underneath." She pulled her swimsuit top out of the straw bag, waved it over her head, and tossed it. The wind caught it and it flew way in the back, too.

I put the car in the gravel for a second, then swerved back on the road.

"Drive much?" she said.

I tried to concentrate better.

Soon a light rain began to fall.

"This thing got a top?" she said.

"Oh, yeah," I said. "You want it up?" The rain was pretty much deflected by the windshield, but we were getting hit with a few drops and I could see where it would be a problem if it fell any more heavily.

I pulled off the road and got out.

I'd never seen my father put up the top. In fact, all the times I'd ridden with him, and all the time we were practicing, it was never an issue, since it hadn't rained. There were a couple of chrome catches, one on each side, and it seemed if you loosened them that would free the top. But I'd get one loose, then go around to get the other, and the first would somehow be caught again.

I did this two or three times, then finally had Carmella get out and hold one open while I released the other. By this time, the rain had started to fall more heavily. I could see the seats were getting wet, now that we were standing still. I started to pull the top up, but it seemed to be stuck, so I pulled harder. Too late I realized that with all the fooling around and opening and closing, the swimsuit bra Carmella had thrown in the back got caught in the hinge on one of the foldout struts. I went around and tried to free it. Meantime, the rain started pouring down.

"Come on, Colm," said Carmella. "*Do* something. I'm getting all wet."

I tried to force the top back down, but the bra was caught in the hinge. I could see a big, black grease smear on it already. I tried to pull it out, but stopped when I heard a tear. I hoped Carmella hadn't heard it, too.

"Look," I told her, "your suit is caught in the top, and I can't get it up. We'll have to get under a bridge or something."

"Just go on," Carmella snapped. "We're not that far."

It was a little better driving, some of the rain bouncing off the windshield so it wasn't quite hitting us in the face, but Carmella stared ahead at the road the whole rest of the way, her hair pasted down on her neck, and never once looked at me.

Rule 9: Don't look back; your wishes may be gaining on you.

Ten

It would take a good sense of humor to get through the rest of the day.

At least one of us had one.

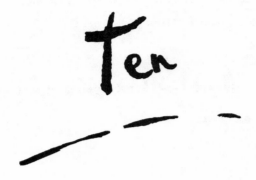

Getting to Barstow Lake all wet wasn't a very good start. Luckily we *had* planned on swimming and, by the time we got there, we had moved out of the storm. It wasn't quite sunny, but it *was* warm enough to put the towels down and lie in the sun a little to dry out. Carmella made do with her blouse for a swimsuit top, unbuttoning a few more buttons, and tying the tails up more tightly under her breasts. When it got wet, she attracted some attention, and that also seemed to cheer her up. Add a little frolicking in the waves and chasing around the beach and the problems getting there were all but forgotten. I tried to stall, but Carmella kept insisting that we go on the rides, so we stowed our stuff in a rental locker and headed off to the amusement area.

First thing off, I bought Carmella some cotton candy, only when she went to bite it, she got a big glob of it caught in her hair. I started laughing, but she gave me a look and stalked off for the bathrooms, coming back with her hair wet again and combed out on one side.

Remember I said how I was kind of a wimp about some of the rides? Well, Carmella was like the twins—nothing seemed to bother her. So I spent the afternoon being spun, whirled, blasted, bumped, squashed, twisted, stretched, and hung. Stick me in the oven for an hour at 350 degrees and I'd have made a good loaf of bread.

In the middle of all this, I made the mistake of eating a chili dog—with cheese and onions, please—which decided it liked this roughhousing less than I did, and refused to stay around for it. By gulping air into my stomach—a trick Marlene had taught me once from her nurse mom—I was able to hold it down, at least until we got off the ride we were on (Loco Motion), when I made it to the trash can and un-ate it.

I tried to be casual, wiping the vomit off my mouth,
going to the men's room and blowing my nose and splashing water on my face, although I could see my skin

had gone mayonnaise white and I was sweating so much, my hair was wet.

"What's the matter with you?" said Carmella. She looked like she was getting worried, although it was the kind of worry like when I was having a good time and the twins were losing it. I was determined to hang on, though, and got her to sit on a bench with me for a few minutes while we drank sodas, figuring since my stomach was now in the trash can, I shouldn't have any more troubles with it. And just as we sit down, who should come sauntering along, buttons open wide showing off his u-shirt, but Dean?

"Car-a-mella!" he said.

"Dean!" she said. Not at all having a problem with two guys meeting who she was dating. "You said you couldn't get off," she threw at him.

He acted as if she didn't say anything. "Who you here with? Hi, Carl," he said, giving me a little backhand flick like when you're trying to get a fly off your french fries.

"Colm," I said.

"Oh, yeah, right," he said. "How did you get here? You got a ride?"

"Colm is driving now," said Carmella. "He's got a car."

"What you got?" he said to me, suddenly interested.

I told him. "It's my dad's, actually," I added.

"Oh, *Ing-leesh*, huh? That the one I saw down by your house?" he said.

"Yeah, I guess," I said.

"Hot," he said, flatly.

"And who are *you* here with?" Carmella said, sounding like one of the twins when they're calling each other "dirt pants."

"Just drove on up by my lonesome," he said. "Guy showed up who I was covering for, so they sent me home. I left work and just kept on driving."

"Here?" she said.

"Your aunt said you were up here."

"Oh, so you stopped at the house first?"

"I was gonna rescue you. You're always bitching about how there's nothing to do. But I guess you found something."

They had started to ignore me, which I wasn't at all disappointed about, feeling the way I was.

"So, have a good time," he said, and turned to go.

"Wait!" said Carmella. "Colm, you sitting this one out?" Here she pointed to some big death machine with spinning cages that was grinding up carcasses behind us.

I nodded.

"You want to go on with me?" she asked Dean. "You don't mind, right, Colm?"

"No, sure," I said, half thankful that Dean was picking up the slack till I recovered.

They had to sit with Carmella in front and Dean in back of her in this little cage, with his legs around her. The thing roared to life, and I didn't even want to look at them getting squashed together.

And somehow, little by little, *my* date with Carmella became *our* date with Carmella. I was going to say "as Dean tagged along," but pretty soon it was clear that I was the one doing the tagging. They had been here so many times, they had their favorite places to eat, and rides to ride and games to play. I kind of felt like I was supposed to be the guy who was pissed that somebody was stealing his girl, except for a few small problems: She was, by nobody's call, "my girl," and he wasn't stealing her. She was, all by herself, paying more attention to him than me. And what was I supposed to be, anyway? Some silverback gorilla in the mist, protecting his breeding female? It was all too . . . obvious. Like some old TV movie my parents watched. Tarzan, King of the Stooges. "Aeeeyouwayeooowawayeooo! Hey, Moe! Get yer hairy mitts offa her!"

Toward late afternoon, it started to cloud up again, and you could see Carmella taking a quick look at the sky every once in a while. Although she didn't say anything, it didn't take much to see what was coming.

As it was getting darkest, Carmella wanted to go on

the merry-go-round and Dean and I weren't so sure.

"You're not going to get sick on the *merry-go-round*,

are you?" she shot at me. She had been trying to be polite all along, but finally dropped even this act.

"Nah," I said, "but we're twice as big as any of the kids on line." Dean nodded, and I thought I had an ally. "And we'll be getting hard looks from their parents," I made the mistake of adding, tilting my head toward the older folks standing there—all baseball caps, beer bellies, and big diaper bags.

"Let's do it, then," said Dean. Remember, Dean is the kind of guy who likes to take up two parking spaces.

We got three horses across, with Dean on the outside, hanging off even before we started spinning. I was on the inside with Carmella between us, and wouldn't you know, turning in that tight circle *did* start to flip my stomach again, even though I worked hard to show I was having just a great time. As we spun faster and faster, I suddenly heard a drumming on the roof and could see people running for cover. The greasy guy running the ride got on the speaker to tell Dean to stop leaning off his horse and he and Carmella had a big laugh about that, and soon after, the ride slowed and stopped. We stood at the edge of the exit area while everyone else pushed past us to find shelter from the rain.

"Colm," said Carmella. "We're going to get soaked if you don't get that roof up."

"Problemos?" said Dean.

Carmella explained the situation.

"Maybe I could help you fix it," he said.

"Let's wait it out some," I said.

And we ran to the restaurant they had in the park, and sipped ice cream sodas as I watched Carmella put her bare, tanned foot on Dean's under the table when she thought I wasn't looking. It had lightened up some by the time we were ready to go, but was still drizzling.

"Come on," said Dean. "I have some tools in my car, maybe I can help you get that top up."

With the rain, many people had already left, so Dean was able to move his car to a space next to ours. He opened his car's passenger door and Carmella got in. She started looking around.

"Dean, did you ever find my comb?" she said.

"Yeah," he said, "it was stuck down in the backseat. I put it in the glove compartment."

She took it out and began fixing her hair in the vanity mirror on back of the visor, and listening to the radio. Dean opened the trunk and took out a canvas bundle that he unrolled to show a shiny tool kit with pliers, screwdrivers, and a socket wrench with sockets, all in little pockets. He tried to take off the hinge using the socket wrench, but it kept slipping off the nut.

"Must be metric," he said. "Don't have no *Ing-leesh* sockets on me, but I'll do my best."

He took an adjustable wrench to them and I could see the little hold-down nuts were getting stripped, and finally one sheared off. It was plain he wasn't going to be able to get it back together. He did work Carmella's bra free, but there was an ugly tear in one of the cups and a black eye of grease around the hole.

"I guess I can kiss that good-bye," she said, as he held the bra up for her to see.

"Put it on, and I'll do it for you," said Dean.

She rolled her eyes, but you could see she liked it.

Dean and I were starting to get pretty wet as the rain picked up to a drizzle. The top now seemed permanently stuck down.

"Sorry," he said. "I guess I ain't going to be able to help you-all." And he rolled up his tools and put them under his arm and put his hands in his pockets.

"Colm," said Carmella, "I don't want to get all wet again. Would you mind so very much if Dean drove me back?"

What could I say?

"Come over here," she said. I went over to the window of the car. She motioned me with her finger to bend down to where she was sitting. "Give me a call when you get home," she whispered in my ear, and gave me a Hollywood kiss on the cheek. Dean slammed down the trunk lid and slid in next to her. She didn't give him much room. Soon I was standing in the lot, watching the taillights of his car blink out as he took off from the stop sign at the exit.

Nothing left but to get the car back home, and think

of a way to explain to Dad how I screwed up the top, not to mention getting the inside—seats, dashboard, carpets, steering wheel, radio, glove compartment, shift stick, pedals—Did I leave anything out?—all wet. All this after driving home drenched and miserable, looking like an idiot sitting in the rain in the Ing-leesh tin-can car.

I'm sure you've figured out by now that when things are going bad, you have to be extra careful, since bad things tend to string themselves together? And sorry if I wasn't all that sharp right now. And maybe it was the rain falling in my face, or something still erupting in the remains of my stomach, or maybe it was grief about blowing it with Carmella, and I'm sure it was the fact that it was getting dark and the road was slippery, and there were all these orange barrels and reflectors in the lane next to me, but here I am tooling along, the rain pouring off me, trying to look natural like I *want* the damn top down, and I start to merge over, since it looks like the lane I'm in is closed off by the barrels up ahead. But I guess I forget advisory number 1374.04—"You could hide a truck in what you can't see in the mirror"—and don't turn my head. Next there's a horn blaring in my ear, and I instinctively jerk the wheel to get away from it, and then there's a barrel right in front of me and, for an all-too-long second, I forget whether I'm driving the Hog or the rental or Dad's car or what, and I do a little dance until I get the pedals right, but by now, I'm right on top of a whole row of the barrels, and I mow a few of them down, reflectors flying all over the place and I'm skidding off and into some goddam *trench* they're digging, and the car goes down *hard*.

I sit there for a few seconds, gaping down into blackness, and feeling myself all over to make sure I still have all my major limbs. Unfortunately for me, I do. I promised my dad I'd wear the seat belt, and here I am, another miracle poster child saved by it, so my dad could have the satisfaction of killing me himself. When I pop open the clasp, I kind of fall out of the belt, the car is at such an angle. Stumbling around in the gravel and dirt, I see right away, it's terminal. The fancy fender is crinkled back into the wheel, which gives new meaning to the word "flat," and a green liquid is oozing out from under the hood and dripping off the front bumper and into the dirt.

There's no way I'm going anywhere.

The guy with the station wagon stops almost right away—"You OK?"—and then I'm swallowed up in the mass of sweaty, sandy kids, the sloppy, fish-fragrant mutt taking my picture with his rear. The guy drops me off a half mile from home. When I finally drag myself in, the house is dark. I can't imagine where everyone's gone. I sit down on the couch on the porch and put my head in my hands.

What to do?

Curse my luck?

Laugh?
Cry?
Think?
I'm too confused to even know.

Rule 10: "Things can't get much worse" is often more a wish than a statement of fact.

Eleven

I sat like this for I don't know how long.

The house got darker and darker.

Where could everyone be?

It was hot and damp and after a while I thought I'd sit out by the lake. I put on my swimsuit and a T-shirt, walked out back, and sat cross-legged on the scrubby beach behind the house. I could see flashes of heat lightning and hear rumblings in the distance.

Dad would *really* be pissed now. His shiny new want-a-woman-wagon destroyed; sitting out on the highway somewhere, open to the elements. I knew he was particular and wouldn't want to call just *anyone* to go tow it. I mean, it *was* English and who knew? He would have ideas about who was best and how it should be done, so in the meantime there was nothing much I could do that would be right.

Then the thought hit me that maybe it *couldn't* be fixed and was wrecked for good, like a stepped-on butterfly, or worse, like my father's trust in me. He let me use something that was very valuable to him—I couldn't help believe that it was really some kind of a test—and I screwed up. Now he'd really be convinced that I could never make it, that there was no hope for me. Worse than that, I thought he might be onto something: Maybe I *should* give it up.

And on top of that, *I* had been getting used to the idea of losing a father, and probably could get used to it again. But Mom? I knew there'd be enough muddy blame splattering around that some would get on her, and all this would push Dad away from her even when they were only starting to get back together.

And Carmella?

And Marlene?

And the stars?

And even more than all this, like the rumbling of a freight train you suddenly notice off in the distance, was the feeling that I screwed up the best chance I had so far in figuring out the real rules to this thing, and was as far away from finding them as ever.

Maybe farther.

I mean, here I was going to be a goddam *senior* in high school when I got back, and I didn't know any more about dating and girls and driving and all the rest of it and was probably worse off than some lowly freshman. And how was it that most adults, with all their years of living on this planet, couldn't tell me about getting along, going along, getting through, or anything else very useful in any recognizable form, and on top of that, were throwing things in my way instead?

The lake by this time of the summer was warm, and I peeled off my shirt as I waded in, tossing it back on the beach. I cleared a path through the reeds, then splashed in all the way. This was something I could understand, this whole warm, friendly bulk of the lake out here in the dark. It didn't scare me a bit, despite all the tales and myths and superstitions and dumb ideas people had about it. I mean, I should know it as well as anyone, with all the time I spent in it. I also remembered something else my dad told me when I was a kid and first learning to swim: "Don't be scared of deep water," he said. "You can drown in a bathtub. Remember that when the water is deep, it only means there's more of it to hold you up." And that's what I felt like, comfortable, like I was on a giant, soft water bed, floating on my back in the dark. Although I don't think I put it into conscious thought until much later, I was soothed by the feeling that at least there was some stability in the universe: At least this would be here to hold me up when all else failed.

As I floated, the breeze brought the fresh ozone

smell of rain to my nose. I could see out of the corner of my eye that the lightning was flashing closer, but I could still barely hear the rumbles, and I knew it was still far off, and likely to stay that way given how storms usually kept their distance.

I flipped over and took a few strokes. All the tension seemed to flow out of my body almost right away as my muscles felt the familiar pulls. I stroked along for a little while like this, getting the rhythm going: *Over with the right arm, blow in the water, pull through, thrust out with the left, keep the hand cupped, head tilted, suck in the warm, wet air, left hand now pulls, flutter-kick through it all like the slap of windshield wipers, rhythmically happening somewhere else* . . . like a mental chant.

It had been a week or so since I'd been in the water and I felt amazingly light and strong. For me, by now, swimming was as easy as walking and a lot more satisfying. I just kept pushing armloads of water behind me, sliding through, maybe the closest that people ever come to feeling like they're flying.

I was getting out pretty far. No matter, this side of the lake was shallow, and I could always roll on my back and float if I got winded, and I was nowhere near that. I took a quick look behind me. The yard where Carmella taught me those first few dance steps was bright as a stage, but like after the show is over and they bring the lights up, and you get that kind of sad feeling to see that it's all plywood and painted cloth. Everyone was probably in the garage with it looking like rain again.

And Carmella?

It was pretty clear that I was her boy toy. Just a weekend stand-in when somebody better wasn't around. I was something to pass the time: television you could touch—in spite of that night out under the stars and the stuff at the movie and the kiss on the beach and all the rest of it. And I saw that this was something like what I'd wanted with *her,* too. What *did* we have in common, after all? What was *really* there? And right then I had the feeling you get when you wake up from a dream where you've just blown a big test—forgot all about it—and it's such a relief to see the sun coming in the actual window of your actual bedroom. It suddenly hit me that with Marlene I could see she was a *real* person who I had some *real* feelings for, instead of—what? Something I *thought* I wanted?

I plodded along in a relaxed kind of way, glancing back to keep in line with the small patch of brightness to keep myself from swimming in circles. I could see the little yard getting smaller and smaller still. I began to wonder how I could ever have made so much of such a tiny thing. I thought this is how my dad must've felt, swimming out of his old life and into his new.

The breeze—more of a light wind by now—had started to come up good and felt refreshing. When I had my mouth up out of the water for the few seconds of each stroke, it blew away any drops of water I might have sucked in, and gave me all the more reason to keep going.

I don't know exactly when it was that it hit me that I would swim to the other shore. Maybe it was when I thought I was so far along that it would probably be just as easy to go on as to double back. If I ever had any doubts about it they blew right on through, and there it was: I was going to swim the lake.

The fact that I'd never made it more than halfway didn't bother me. And that I was probably near the point where I'd crapped out before wasn't troubling either since I had no—not even a beginning—sense of fatigue. And the farther I went, the less my problems seemed to weigh on me: My mom turning away as my dad pulled up, the twins with ice cream dripping down their faces, my dad scowling at me as I tried to gun the car over the pothole, Carmella smiling her little smile, eyes sparkling in the lantern light, Dean smirking as he walked past me to get in his car with Carmella, Marlene looking hurt after how I treated her at the raft, Uncle Junior grimacing as he hauled his leg up under him; they all seemed suddenly as small and far away as that dimly lit yard way behind me. It was like I was floating up in the air and could see all of them down there, dotted lines leading from them, showing where they were going to go next, like some diagram of their lives—some sort of board game, like Monopoly or something, where it all didn't really matter that much, anyhow. When the first few serious splashes of rain hit my face, it was like they snapped me out of a dream, and with them, I began to notice the first signs of tiredness.

Even this was no matter, I'd felt it many times before. What do you think all those laps in all those pools were about? Workouts didn't really start until the hurt and fatigue cut in. Alfieri liked to say that the pain was your ally: Since *everyone* felt it, if you worked hard enough, you would learn to tolerate it better and then it would become a strength—an advantage you could take over someone who let it get in their way. So when you were so tired you didn't kick enough to get your mouth clear and you took in water, so did they, and when you could choke and get on with it and they couldn't, you were ahead.

And even when the rain started heavy so that the wind no longer did any good, and when I tried to get air I was breathing half water, I still pumped on, finding that place inside, that small place of concentration that was beyond whatever it was that was synching all those muscles in this dance of motion: beyond the strain, beyond the burn, keeping me just hung on that edge where you quit, seeing I only needed to let go to let myself comfortably fall off, but seeing I could just as well keep going.

By now the little lit yard was so far behind I couldn't

even see it, and all the other dots of light around the lake had started to wink on and off with the sheets of rain knifing through the air and getting in my eyes. But then, a tremendous flash suddenly threw everything into blue-black light and shadow. I saw I was tending toward one side and corrected, trying to get a glimpse of what was in front, to find *something* ahead I could recognize; some sight of land. Next, a huge blast of thunder swallowed me up, startling me so I got a burst of adrenaline and flew through the next few strokes like one of those cartoon characters who's being chased by a shark, and windmills so hard he comes up out of the water. At one time, that much adrenaline would have overwhelmed me, made me trembly and weak like when you get out of a too hot bath, but I'd learned to work through it, too, and get it behind me, so it pushed me even harder. It wasn't such a good idea, I knew, being out on the lake in a lightning storm, but I was virtually one with the water by now, slipstreaming below the chop so I didn't think I made any kind of a good target anyway. The flashes and blasts came closer and closer together now. With each burst of light, I tried to get a better fix on where I was headed, but the rain was too heavy. It was like putting on headlights in a thick fog—all I saw was the light shining off the water pouring down around me. Now I knew I was starting to lose it. This was beyond, *way* beyond anything I'd ever done. Even in a practice, when you took sets of wind sprints at the end, you could hold onto the side of the pool for a while after. I had never made such a sustained straight effort before.

I sensed I was getting into what I figured was the deeper end of the lake, beginning to hit little eddies as cold as pump water, where the springs bubbled in from way underground somewhere—probably the same icy aquifer we tapped with the Hog. *I could see the Hog now, resting on the bottom, driving pipe, the weight bobbing up and down in slow motion, big balloons of clammy cold water spewing out of the pipe end. My dad working the rig, telling me to go home and give up since I wasn't any help. I looked for Uncle Junior, but . . . There he was. Up near the rigging, floating gracefully now, his leg more useful than when it miserably tried to haul him around on land, pointing to the entrance to what looked like a cavern, waving me away from it. I could feel now the icy stream spilling out of the cavern as if from some great underground river that ended up here, flowing thousands of miles under the earth. It must have been carrying some dirt out with it, too, because I was finding it harder and harder to shove my way through. For moles and sandworms it must be like swimming, but it wasn't like water you could just push aside. It was like being stuck in wet sand with the stupid pail on my head—I had to get up out of it. Who cared if the twins cried? You couldn't hold me down like this, like I was still some little kid, my arms and legs in casts, who just had to take it. If I could just get it off me—break out of it. If I could—*

And then I saw it: There was a flash of lightning and in its intense stab of light, I could see it bearing down on me.

The white canoe!

The next flash and I saw a girl, in buckskin, her hair braided, scooping the water with her paddle, single-mindedly coming at me, above me, down here on water level as I was, and gaining. I had to get away, and I squeezed out another dozen or so strokes, beyond my exhaustion, wringing out every molecule of energy that was in me. Then I saw that instead of running me down, the canoe began running alongside, and then pulling slightly ahead, and I knew she was with me, supporting me. I felt somehow serene in knowing this, and in giving over to this oneness of purpose—me and the girl pulling together—I found a peacefulness that put me in a place beyond the pain. And, as the rain peaked and let up, and the flashes of lightning grew less and less blinding, I saw that the canoe wasn't white after all, but a dull shade of brownish gray-green.

Suddenly the water wasn't holding me up as well anymore. It had somehow gone thin, more like air, so that when I pulled, there wasn't as good a move forward, and this exhausted me all the more. My arms began slapping the water like at the end of a day of double workouts with my dad and Alfieri, but then on one of these slap-and-drags, my right hand hit something hard. I got my legs under me and stood, bent over and gasping, water still streaming from my hair into my mouth as I gulped in air, stumbling up and crashing onto the beach—a land creature after all.

I heard the canoe scrape onto land at my feet, and I sat up, suddenly chilled by the wet breeze that had come down behind the storm.

"You did it," cried Marlene, as she jumped out and pulled her canoe up on the beach. "You swam the whole damn lake!" She ran up and hugged me. Her sweatshirt was wet from the rain, but I could feel her warmth through it. I held onto her and somehow our faces wound up together and, next thing I knew—I think it was as much a surprise to her as to me—we kissed.

Rule 11: True friends find you when you need them the most.

Twelve

Did I tell you everything would come out all right in the end?

Well, I guess I was lying again.

My dad was *monumentally* pissed. That is, once he got over the crazy idea that he was happy I wasn't dead. Mom and Dad and the twins had all gone down to the Pacettis'. Left me a note, which I didn't see. Right on the refrigerator the whole time, of course, big as a bedsheet. Maybe if I had turned on a light . . .

My mom told me later that, at first, they got nervous when I didn't show at dinner. Then, as it got later, Dad got more and more angry. Then Carmella, who blew in after they ate, said how the top on the car was wrecked, and Dean drove her back and then he really started steaming. They figured any minute, I guess, I'd come slinking on down there, wearing a black plastic garbage bag and whipping myself with a busted-off car aerial. And then, when I didn't show at all, they got worried that I had Done Something Drastic! Who Knows What? and they came home.

When they found the house all dark, they pushed the sprint button on the panic treadmill, and my mom was all for calling the cops. My dad, knowing the full wienertude of his son, figured I was just out roaming around trying to build up the nerve to come back. But then they found my shirt on the beach, and thought the worst. Believe me when I tell you I'm not going to kill myself over some dumb car. But they've seen way too many made-for-TV movies. So, even though it was still storming, my dad went to get a boat and go out on the lake looking for me. So they were greatly relieved and angry and grateful and who knows what, when right then, just as Dad was hauling the rowboat out from behind the garage, I showed up in the canoe with Marlene.

It hadn't seemed right to tell them at that very moment that I'd swum the lake, so I only told them I was out with Marlene, talking. My mom hugged me, then held me at arm's length by the shoulders so she could look at me. Tears were running down her face. "We were so, *so* worried, Colm," she said, then hugged me again. Then she couldn't say anything else. The twins needed attention anyway; they were cold and tired and cranky, so she took them in the house. Like I said, Dad was happy to see me at first, but after I told him *all* that had happened to his car, and where it still was, he looked at me—stunned. He looked at me and I thought for a moment he was going to start crying. It was like you could see that behind his eyes he was screening one of his old black-and-white, jerky-action mental movies. This one opening on the peeling housefront and dirt yard of some run-down rental, then panning to *his* father, who looked like he was peeking at another hand much better than the one he was dealt. I guess I hadn't truly realized how much the car meant to Dad—finally thinking he'd get those four aces for himself just this once, but finding the down card was a joker.

Instead of crying, though, he wiped his hand over his face as if he'd surfaced from a pool, turned, and stalked into the house. I almost wish he would've yelled, said *something*. I stood on the shore, looking at the house, my back to the water. Marlene's house was dark. She'd been fearless in the storm on the lake, but slipped away when she saw the storm clouds gathering over my parents' heads, and was probably in bed by now, though I bet she wasn't sleeping.

I picked my shirt up off the beach and dragged it on, unmindful of the wet and sand. I stood for a long while, facing the house, until I heard a truck pull up in front and saw yellow flashing lights burst through the trees like a flash fire. I heard doors open and close, and the squawk of the truck radio and people talking. Then the truck pulled off. In the quiet that was left, I could hear the crickets going, and an occasional frog erupting down in the reeds behind me.

Inside the house, the twins had fallen asleep on the couch and my mom had carried them into their bunk beds. She finished tucking them in and came out on the porch to say good night.

"Where is he?" I asked.

"He had the tow truck pick him up. He wants to see for himself. We're just glad you're all right, Colm," she said. Then she said she was exhausted, kissed me on the forehead one more time, and went off to bed.

I sat out on the back porch and looked at the lake. Its surface was strangely still, despite the chill breeze that followed the rain, and you could see reflected in it the disk of the moon sliding through the scuddy clouds. About a half hour later, I heard the truck pull up again, complete with the sound and light show of before, and then grind off. I could hear my father's footsteps on the walk, the front door open and close, and then his slow tread through the house all the way to the porch door behind me. I didn't turn around. I was hoping he was just waiting for a radio cab, or was going back in to sleep on the living room sofa.

"It's not as bad as I thought," he said quietly. "They think a new front strut and a tire and headlamp and a little body work on the fender. You must've been going pretty slow." I thought of all the cars passing me. "They don't know about the interior. I'll have to check that out in daylight."

"Dad," I said, turning toward him, "I'm really sorry. I know how much that car meant to you." He looked older again, standing there backlit by the yellow light of the dining room lamp. I started to say something about how I should have been more careful.

"No, no, Colm." He cut me off.

"But, Dad . . ." I started to say.

"Things happen," he said, then was quiet for a long time. "It can't all be perfect. It can't all come out how we like it."

He put his hand on my shoulder and I winced, thinking he was going to call me "son" again. But he didn't. "You know what they told me?" he said as if he suddenly thought of something else. "The tow truck guys?"

"No," I said.

"That from what they could see, it wasn't the first time the car was wrecked. So it was never perfect to begin with," he said. "Just like most things."

Then he stood to go back in the house. I stood too and then, wonder of wonders, he pulled me to him in a great big bear hug. Imagine! My own dad, joining the ranks of Men Who Hug. Then, instead of the cab or the couch, he said "Good night," knocked on my mom's bedroom door, and as if she were waiting up for him, I heard her say, "Come in."

I guess at the Pacettis', and afterward, when they found my shirt on the beach, Dad and Mom had plenty of time to worry. And although worrying together isn't the same as love, it's a start.

And as for them getting back together, who knows? I wish I could give you a happy ending here. But it took a lot, over a long time, for things to come apart. It's going to take a lot, over a long time, for them to get back together. If they ever do. Rome wasn't built on water, you know.

School would start in a few days, and we began getting everything packed up. The Pacettis had us beat by twenty-four hours, once again piling everything into and on top of their cars and caravanning off one Saturday morning, not long after all this. Uncle Junior went back to his caretaking, and I was, once again, jobless. He took me for a ride one night to say good-bye for the summer.

"Well, what do you think about working for a living?" he asked as we rode around the lake in the Buick, past the boarded-up ice cream place, with the SEE YOU NEXT SUNDAE sign, and the barricaded beach roads.

"It's good," I said. "I like it that I have a little money to buy my own shoes, or a haircut."

"Your wreck didn't wipe you out?"

"No, my dad said to forget it, but I want to make it up anyway. I said I'd pay him back little by little, as I earned it. It's important to me."

"Yeah," he said. "One of the pluses of having your own cash: You don't have to put up with someone who's got something on you. You going back swimming again in school?"

"I don't think so," I said. "I've got nothing to prove."

"But that's the best reason," he said. "Now you can do it on your own terms."

"If they'll take me," I said. "I'll have to think about it. How's Carmella?" I asked.

"Oh, yeah, she said to say hello," he said. "And asked why you didn't call."

I shrugged.

"And old Dean-boy?" I asked.

"History," he said. "She's got some new character she met in the city. But hey, she's young, and if I looked that good . . ." He let it trail off.

"Next summer?" he said when we got back. "I'll be doing the well-drilling gig again, and I'll need someone."

"I'll let you know," I said. I didn't have a plan for next week, never mind next year.

I'd be lying to you all the more if I said that I still felt something for Carmella. After everything that happened at Barstow it somehow just disappeared. You know, like the way gum is great when you first put it in your mouth, but after a while you get that awful taste and say, "Why am I chewing this stuff?"

One thing I *do* know is that Marlene, in addition to being there when I *really* needed her, was the only one I could actually share swimming the lake with. She understood it in an unspoken way all along. My mom, of course, thought it was dumb from the beginning. And Dad, when I finally told him, would have said the strain wasn't worth it, and that a well-planned, extended workout would have done a lot more good for me. That's what his old critical *past* self would have said, anyway. In fact he didn't really say much at all except that it was great that I did it, and didn't I think I should have quit when the lightning started? The twins were too little to connect all the dots. And Uncle Junior? He just patted his bum leg, which hung useless from the seat of the car. "Yeah, I know," he said. "There comes a point where you got to size up your strengths and limits and just decide to do what you got to." But with all he'd done in his life . . . I really don't think it seemed like that much to him.

But Marlene had been there and was there, and no matter how dumb it seemed, she knew how important it was to me, and how important that I do it on my own terms.

And that kiss?

Now, I know you've seen them thousands of times on TV and in the movies and in comic books and magazines and on billboards and cereal boxes, and gum wrappers, and in films about mammals they show you in school, but this one was different. It wasn't all strings coming up on the sound track and waves crashing over sleek bodies in the surf. And it wasn't like those weird kinds of things that happen to two people's mouths when they think they're supposed to kiss because they're going out. No, this came from inside somewhere and wasn't anything you could have planned, and felt just fine, like two people getting together. Like the most natural thing in the world.

So what have I learned from all this? Well, in spite of what TV and all that other stuff tells you, that hot, desirous feeling like I had with Carmella isn't really everything. Oh, don't get me wrong. It feels good. Don't ever let anybody tell you it doesn't. And it's real. But it's like eating a whole bag of taco chips. You know how you're full, but you're not? You see, the problem is that this person you have these feelings for is still a *person*, with habits and faults and everything. You may find out that although you might think you *love* her, you might not *like* her. And that's a real feeling, too. But this is the next step to figure—something they don't tell you about—how do you make these two things work together? Love somebody so you have that rush, but at the same time like them as a real person?

It's part you and part them, I know this much. And in the end, it's nothing anyone can teach you.

But then, why am I telling you this? It's like I said, you have to learn it all for yourself, anyway. This is as much as I know. Tune in seventy years from now, and I'll tell you how it all comes out.

And the stars?

They're still up there, of course. Can't see them in the city with all the lights. But I still got that dizzy caffeine high when Marlene and I watched them from a bluff overlooking the lake the night before I left. And I expect they'll keep their kick when I visit her on weekends. But there was something else there too. I don't know how to describe it. Something that wouldn't fit in a sitcom. Something you get only from living your own life. It was like the way I felt floating in the lake—a kind of quiet wonder—a contentment that life has some great things in store if you can only stay real and be attentive enough. And in its own constant and reliable way, I'm learning to appreciate how it's so much better than what they try to tell you.

At least it's a solid place to start.

Rule 12: There are no rules.